THE
Reinvention
OF MOXIE
Roosevelt

ELIZABETH CODY KIMMEL

PUFFIN BOOKS
An Imprint of Penguin Group (USA) Inc.

PUFFIN BOOKS

Published by the Penguin Group

Penguin Young Readers Group, 345 Hudson Street, New York, New York 10014, U.S.A.

Penguin Group (Canada), 90 Eglinton Avenue East, Suite 700, Toronto, Ontario, Canada M4P 2Y3
(a division of Pearson Penguin Canada Inc.)

Penguin Books Ltd, 80 Strand, London WC2R 0RL, England

Penguin Ireland, 25 St Stephen's Green, Dublin 2, Ireland (a division of Penguin Books Ltd)

Penguin Group (Australia), 250 Camberwell Road, Camberwell, Victoria 3124, Australia
(a division of Pearson Australia Group Pty Ltd)

Penguin Books India Pvt Ltd, 11 Community Centre, Panchsheel Park, New Delhi - 110 017, India

Penguin Group (NZ), 67 Apollo Drive, Rosedale, Auckland 0632, New Zealand
(a division of Pearson New Zealand Ltd.)

Penguin Books (South Africa) (Pty) Ltd, 24 Sturdee Avenue,
Rosebank, Johannesburg 2196, South Africa

Registered Offices: Penguin Books Ltd, 80 Strand, London WC2R 0RL, England

First published in the United States of America by Dial Books for Young Readers,
a division of Penguin Young Readers Group, 2010
Published by Puffin Books, a division of Penguin Young Readers Group, 2011

1 3 5 7 9 10 8 6 4 2

THE LIBRARY OF CONGRESS HAS CATALOGED THE DIAL BOOKS FOR YOUNG READERS EDITION AS FOLLOWS:

Kimmel, Elizabeth Cody

The reinvention of Moxie Roosevelt / by Elizabeth Cody Kimmel.

p. cm.

Summary: On her first day of boarding school, a thirteen-year-old girl who feels boring and
invisible decides to change her personality to match her unusual name.

ISBN 978-0-8037-3303-9 (hc)

[1. Personality—Fiction. 2. Self-perception—Fiction.
3. Boarding schools—Fiction. 4. Schools—Fiction.] I. Title.

PZ7.K56475Re 2010

[Fic]—dc22

2009037939

Puffin Books ISBN 978-0-14-241870-3

Text set in Bembo

Printed in the United States of America

A fresh start!

What was freaking me out was the fact that here it was at last—my big chance to start over. I was going to a new school where no one knew anything about me. I was a blank slate. For that first day, for those first few weeks, I would have the opportunity to reinvent myself completely.

I see it like one of those reality shows where a team rushes in and rips a bunch of stuff out of your house and completely redesigns it with new stuff in a Unified Look. Except on *my* reality show, instead of my house it would be me that got the makeover—inside and out. The team of experts would change me from a regular person into someone who stood out.

So I had a plan. But I had never taken the time to work out the details. Graduation sort of snuck up on me. Summer flew by even without camp eating up the days. I hung out with the other music nerds, complaining and practicing and comparing notes on our plans. None of them were going to boarding school. I had Eaton to myself.

Now I mulled things over anxiously as I sat in the back of our station wagon, luggage piled high, speeding toward my future personality as my parents made cheerful conversation in the front seat. We weren't much more than fifteen miles from the Eaton campus, which meant that I had less than a half hour to decide who I was going to be.

OTHER BOOKS YOU MAY ENJOY

For Spinky

CHaPter one

What goes through people's heads when they come up with names for their kids? Mine, for example. You should be sitting for this. And a deep cleansing breath. Ready?

My full name is Moxie Roosevelt Kipper. In addition to being a mouthful, and a name I will have to spell out for people for the rest of my life, this is a difficult name to live up to. On my very first day of kindergarten, my teacher took attendance, and when she got to the *K*s, her face lit up and she said, "Moxie Roosevelt Kipper—oh my—and who belongs to this very big name?" And when I stood up, all small and ordinary, her face sort of fell—just for a second, before she replaced it with a huge kindergarten-teacher smile. But the message had been received. People expected something when they heard my wacky name, and to date, I have been unable to deliver. I blame my mother and father.

My parents claimed my name was charming, unique, and perfectly represented our family. My father, who's a soda company executive, picked Moxie. Apparently, back in the dim and misty, before TV and basic life-sustaining technology like Internet and cell phones, there was a caffeine- and sugar-packed soda called Moxie. It was sort of a prehistoric version of Red Bull or something. Gave you a nice little lift. And if you were the kind of person who had lots of zip or energy or stood out in some way, people would say "You've got moxie."

This Moxie has no moxie.

Because he cannot be a normal father and collect sports paraphernalia or car magazines, my dad collects old Moxie bottles and ads. He displays them in a glass case in his office. And so far, I'm the only human addition to his collection. I suppose I should be glad he's not fixated on a different soda, making me Mountain Dew Roosevelt or Dr Pepper Kipper. But forgive me, I just don't feel all steeped in good fortune when it comes to the name department.

My mother picked the Roosevelt part. She runs an

Internet grassroots political organization called It's Time. She spends her morning yelling at the newspaper, and has devoted half her life to weeding out corrupt politicians (weeding them out from WHAT I do not know). She spends the other half of her life attempting to direct our country's resources to assist the needy. Apparently, I am named after not just one Roosevelt, but two of them. First, for President Franklin Delano Roosevelt, because of his social programs to help the poor. Second, for President Theodore Roosevelt, because of his character and integrity, in spite of the fact that he was a Republican (which my mom insists doesn't count because he joined the Progressive party before the election).

Again, you might think I should be counting my lucky stars that she didn't insist on naming me Moxie T. Roosevelt-FDR Kipper, just to be accurate. I'm sure she thought about it. But lucky? I don't think so. That two educated people could even agree on such a name for their only daughter is tragic and perplexing.

I have spent thirteen years as Moxie Roosevelt Kipper, each one of them more ordinary than the last. There were only eighty-seven kids at my old school, and everybody knew which of them were future criminals, or bordering on genius, or hysterically eccentric, or dangerously unpredictable.

I was none of these things. There was no name for the kind of kid I was, because other than being able to play the piano, I wasn't much of anything at all.

Here's a little story. About halfway through last year, a bunch of kids snuck into the faculty room and trashed it with toilet paper and shaving cream. They wrote comments—some of them not so nice—on the walls with Silly String. And the principal made this gigantic, huge deal about it, like they were going to bring in the FBI or something.

Most of my class was totally freaking out. Everyone was huddled in little vibrating clusters, worried that they would be questioned, or worse, busted. That it would go on their Permanent Record. That it would Affect Their Entire Future. There was this huge sense of camaraderie about it all.

I made the mistake of joining one of these conversations—I made some comment about how yeah, man, I'm really scared they're going to call me into the principal's office. And everybody just kind of looked at me like I was a kitten dressed up in a cute outfit. Then this one girl Gretchen said, "Oh Mox, you don't need to worry. They're looking for *troublemakers*."

I should have said something about how I *was* a troublemaker—I just never got caught. But I didn't. I couldn't make the words come out of my mouth, which made me furious. It was easy for Gretchen to talk, after all. She had a solid troublemaking reputation. Not one month earlier she had tried to roll the grand piano out of the music room as a practical joke, and accidentally snapped one of its legs off. She practically had a parole officer.

It's not that I *want* people to think I'm a criminal. It's just . . . I don't want them to automatically *assume* I'm not one. Basically, nothing had changed since that first day of kindergarten. It made me nuts. I had to go straight to the music room and pound out some Chopin. I count it as bitterly ironic that I was playing on the very same piano that had lost a leg to Gretchen's practical joke. Some things can only be solved by playing finger-eating waltzes at lightning speed on a grand piano with the lid up. Which basically lays out my geekdom for you right there.

Actually, geekdom would have been an improvement. My problem was invisibility. I felt like I always ended up flying under people's radar. You know, like when you know everything about someone, and apparently they don't recall having even met you? Like last summer, which was my last year at Camp Migawam. I was finally in the oldest group of girls. That summer we had a daytime program exchange going on with the boys' camp across the lake for a boat-building project. Ten boys canoed over to our side of the lake every day to hammer and saw, and the finest one of all was named Carson McGillion. Blue eyes, dimples. The works. I adored him. Well, everybody did. Especially Daphne Anderson, who had very blond hair she wore in super-high, non-age-appropriate pigtails, which the boys liked to tug.

So imagine my surprise when I ran into Carson McGillion at the Space Museum that fall. I decided there was no point in being a wallflower during this very brief window of opportunity, so I walked right up to him. I planned to say: "Hey Carson! It's so cool to see you again—how've you been?" But I ended up just standing there looking at him with my mouth open like I was trying to catch my breath. And his eyes got very wide and you could see the mental grasping going on behind them. In short, Carson McGillion had no idea in France who I was or why I was standing there showing him my tonsils. I'd been just another face in the crowd at boat-building. You can bet if I was Daphne Anderson coyly bouncing a couple of pigtails around, Carson McGillion would have remembered me.

So I realized that one day, when I got out of this little school, I was going to have to do something about my personality. Change it to something that really stood out, like my name—unusual, a bit outlandish, unexpected, sassy.

Finally, my chance had come. I was leaving for boarding school.

This was not as exotic as it might sound. Like I said, I wasn't a genius or a budding criminal. I didn't come from a stupendously wealthy family that tossed bundles of cash on the fire when there was no wood around. And no, I wasn't the orphaned child of profoundly gifted wizards, nor had the living embodiment of evil Who Shall Not Be Named ever at any time tried to kill me but only succeeded in scarring my forehead. Nope, I was just a regular girl going to a regular boarding school. Except that everything I knew about boarding school came from the Harry Potter books. Try as I might to imagine the reality of what lay ahead, I kept coming up with scenes of Sorting Hats and Dementors. In other words, I was pretty unprepared.

It's not like I hadn't known this day was coming. My family lived in the boondocks of the boondocks. Pine Point, New Hampshire. If a person developed a sudden craving for a Twinkie or the latest issue of *Fabulous* magazine at my house, it was a twenty-five-minute drive to the nearest minimart. Our local school only went through the seventh grade. After that, the public school for our district was in a city called Pildrake. It's a forty-mile back-road commute, twice a day, to a school with so many students, the entire building could probably secede from the United States and establish its own zit-covered nation.

So my classmates and I had always known that come seventh grade, we were going to have to make some choices. In a school where the graduating class is eighteen kids, that year's numbers broke down like this: nine students commuting to Pildrake; two students relocating to their divorced dads; four students attending private day school complete with three-and-a-half-hour round trip bus time; two kids being homeschooled; and . . . me. Boarding school.

It's called Eaton Academy for Girls. The admissions brochure made it look like a picture-perfect film location from a Victorian movie shoot. All stone and towers, gargoyles and stained glass. It wasn't far from the high-tech dentist who performed my root canal when I was ten, so I'd actually been driven by it. Mostly what I remembered were the high gates surrounding it, and the vague suggestion of Gothic buildings in the mist. To be honest, it had looked more like Willy Wonka's chocolate factory than an educational institution for girls. But I was only in the fifth grade then, and it never occurred to me that Eaton might be a part of my future.

I was somewhat freaked out about leaving home, though I'd worked through many of my homesickness issues in my five summers at Camp Migawam. I had logged plenty of hours sobbing my way through the night in my cabin, and trying to pretend the noises I was making were all caused by mold and pollen allergies. Eventually I got used to the place. By the time Carson McGillion came along, I was mostly free of the nighttime weepies. Not that he apparently noticed either way. Hopefully it would take considerably less than five years for me to adjust to Eaton. I had promised myself that when a snappy comment came to mind, I would say it out loud, and never stand silently with my mouth open. Plus, I knew for a fact that they had a whole network of practice rooms and a Bosendorfer concert grand piano in the music wing, so I knew where I'd be heading if things got to be too much.

Music was one of the main reasons I was going to Eaton. They were offering me a generous music scholarship, partly because of a piano competition in which I earned top ranking for my interpretation of ten of Bach's Goldberg Variations. I had played them during my admissions interview for Eaton's head of music, Mr. Tate, an Alabama native with a shock of wild white hair. I had warmed to him on sight, and he offered me the scholarship on the spot. So school was practically paid for (which left my parents money to pay for the important things in life, like vintage Moxie bottles and Million Mom March tickets, and my college fund, I guess). And the campus was only about seventy-five miles from home. So theoretically I could escape to my house for the occasional weekend, if I wanted. Plus my parents had stressed repeatedly that we'd be doing Eaton on a trial basis. If it was really awful, I'd homeschool the rest of the year while we rethought our options.

What was freaking me out was the fact that here it was at last—my big chance to start over. I was going to a new school where no one knew anything about me. I was a blank slate. If the faculty room at Eaton suffered from Redecoration by Silly String, I'd be as much a suspect as anyone else. For that first day, for those first few weeks, I would have the opportunity to reinvent myself completely.

I see it like one of those reality shows where a team rushes in and rips a bunch of stuff out of your house and completely redesigns it with new stuff in a Unified Look. Except on *my* reality show, instead of my house it would be me that got the makeover—inside and out. The team of experts would change me from a regular person into someone who stood out. Someone unpredictable and effervescent, who spoke her mind (or someone's mind). A girl you would expect to have a totally unique, vintage name. My reality show would be called *The Reinvention of Moxie Roosevelt*.

So I had a plan. But I had never taken the time to work out the details. Graduation sort of snuck up on me. Summer flew by even without camp eating up the days. I hung out with the other music nerds, complaining and practicing and comparing notes on our plans. None of them were going to boarding school. I had Eaton to myself.

Now I mulled things over anxiously as I sat in the back of our station wagon, luggage piled high, speeding toward my future personality as my parents made cheerful conversation in the front seat. We weren't much more than fifteen miles from the Eaton campus, which meant that I had less than a half hour to decide who I was going to be.

Some of the top contenders:

Mysterious Earth Goddess:
Wears tie-dye and thrift-shop hippie fare, and drops mysterious hints about encounters with the supernatural. Burns incense where permitted. Keeps deck of Tarot cards in hobo bag. Refers frequently to past life experiences. (Some shopping required.)

Hale and Hearty Sports Enthusiast:
Jogs religiously. Performs calf and hamstring stretches while waiting for class to begin. Is depressed or elated depending on status of favorite professional baseball/basketball/football team.

Participates in at least two after-school sports programs. Has copy of *The Encyclopedia of Fitness* in bookshelf. (Considerable physical training required.)

Detached, Unique, Coolly Knowing Individual:
Favors faded jeans and vintage rock T-shirts. Never seen without an iPod. Wears sunglasses indoors. Maintains excellent hairstyle without appearing to try. Makes dry and witty comments that crack people up. Knows names and songs of all the latest indie bands. (Current and back issues of *Rolling Stone* and *Filter* required.)

Assertive Revolutionary Activist:
Wears beat-up denim jacket covered in buttons with slogans. When not attending rallies, can be found painting signs to bring to future rallies. Often seen hunched, head in hand, sighing deeply. (Subscription to *New York Times* and *Mother Jones* magazine required.)

I was comparing and contrasting the qualities of Mysterious Earth Goddess (MEG) versus Detached, Unique,

Coolly Knowing Individual (DUCKI) when my mother turned around and said:

"So! There it is!"

There it was indeed. Just ahead lay the iron gates of Eaton Academy, wide-open and inviting us to pass through, like the jaws of a massive mammal. I took a long, deep breath.

The reinvention of Moxie Roosevelt was about to begin.

chapter TWO

We parked in the crammed visitor's lot and followed the signs to the main campus. One minute we were on a gravel path shaded by massive trees, and the next minute we had emerged onto the quadrangle of the campus.

I was mildly stupefied. This place looked EXACTLY like the brochure. I felt as if I'd accidentally tumbled into their photo shoot. In all four directions towered majestic Gothic stone buildings, cheerfully covered with bright green ivy. The sky was so blue and the lawn so perfect, I was afraid to take another step for fear of smudging something. Everywhere I looked, I saw healthy, laughing girls and cheerful, neatly dressed parents. Purple and white balloons had been strung from the lampposts, and a banner hung from a window proclaiming that my fellow new students and I were WELCOME! It looked like some kind of convention for content and well-nourished people.

It had to be a trick.

"Doesn't all this look nice?" asked my father, sweeping his hand toward the vista like Christopher Columbus arriving in the New World.

The sound of his voice reminded me that I had not, in fact, tumbled into a photo shoot. I had arrived at school, and this was my life. Come what may, in a matter of hours my parents were going to leave me there and drive home. My stomach tightened at the thought of being left here alone. The school year was a lot longer than a camp session. I would have to get right to work on my new personality— it would be a good distraction at the very least.

"There are tables set up over there," my mother was saying. "I'll bet that's where we need to go register."

She was wearing her Save the Tundra T-shirt, which looked slightly faded in the glaring sunlight and appeared from some angles to read "Save the Tuna." I felt a sudden flash of irritation. Couldn't she have at least put on a new shirt? She was beaming at me, and her bangs were being blown gently up by the breeze, making her look like a wise and compassionate terrier. I felt twin strands of affection and embarrassment.

The registration tables were set up on the grass outside one of the huge stone buildings with large wooden doors at either end. Cast in shadow and topped by two round towers, the building looked like an Institute for the Criminally Insane—the kind you might read about in a Victorian gothic novel. I hoped it wasn't a dorm.

I walked over to a plump curly-haired girl seated behind the table. She was wearing a badge that said "Registration Helper." Below that was printed the name Lori, which had been crossed out. Something like "Mavis" or "Matrix" had been handwritten underneath it. My first contact with an Eaton student. I had to be careful. I couldn't get too out of control with a new personality while my parents were standing right behind me. I decided to say as little as possible and let my parents think I was just being shy. But as I made eye contact with the Mavix, my expression screamed Detached, Unique, Coolly Knowing Individual.

The girl's hand shot out so quickly, I actually flinched.

"Hello there!" she barked. "Welcome to Eaton"

She sounded like a drill sergeant. I nodded at her, raising one eyebrow. Yeah, good. That was cool. Eyebrow raising was cool. I was DUCKI.

"I'm here to help you register and get you set to go. Okay? Very good. Let's find your packet in the file. Name?"

The Mavix really had a knack for making things sound military. I was half afraid she'd assign me a bunk, then pull out an electric razor to give me a crew cut.

"Moxie Roosevelt Kipper," I said, placing my hand on one hip and giving her an intense gaze. I didn't smile.

"And I'm Gil Kipper," added my father, from behind me. I winced. His name sometimes sounds a little cheesy.

"Dallas Kipper," said my mother. Don't even get me started on hers.

"Very good," said the Mavix, like our family names had just passed some sort of high-level security clearance. She rummaged through the file marked *A–K,* and quickly produced a folder with my name on it.

"Here's your student handbook, a campus map, course book listing, and dorm assignment. You'll be in third-floor Sage, room 303," she said, gesturing toward the Institute for the Criminally Insane. "That's a triple. You'll have two roommates."

I had to struggle to keep my face emotionless. New students had to share their room with another person, I knew. But two? Two roommates? I thought that only happened on sitcoms.

"Your student proctor is Kristen Berry. She's a senior and can help you with any problems that may arise. You'll find her on the hall now, checking new students in and helping everyone get settled. Any questions?"

The Mavix gave me a look that suggested questions meant weakness. I had been planning on asking where the music practice rooms were, and whether you had to sign up in advance for a piano. Now that seemed dweeby. Instead, I shook my head and shifted my gaze to someplace over her right shoulder. Then I shrugged a little so the Mavix would understand that I was cool—so cool, it didn't matter where I roomed, because I'd be transporting all my coolness with me.

"Right, then. Good luck."

Good luck? Did I need it? What did the Mavix know that I didn't?

I showed my parents the folder, then pointed to the Institute for the Criminally Insane.

"My room's in there," I explained, though I knew they'd heard every word the Mavix had said. My mother took the folder from my hands and examined it, like she didn't believe me.

As we started walking toward the building, something suddenly shot out of a third-floor window and plummeted to the ground with a thud. It disappeared in a sea of green ivy.

I glanced at my parents, but neither of them seemed to have noticed the Unidentified Descending Item. Had I not been so devoted to my Detached, Unique, Coolly Knowing persona, I would have gone hunting through the ivy myself to find out what it was. Instead, I thrust both hands into my pockets and sort of ambled along toward the door. Anyone observing me would logically conclude that I was in complete command of the situation, and utterly unruffled by my new surroundings or plummeting objects. Vintage DUCKI.

But once the thought occurred that somebody might be looking at me, I couldn't get the idea out of my head. With the possibility that a score of new students were watching me from their windows through high-powered binoculars, I began to choreograph my every movement for maximum impact. When we were about five feet from the dormitory's oversized wooden door, I paused and indicated the entrance with my head, in case my parents somehow hadn't noticed it. I gazed around nonchalantly, wearing a slightly bemused expression. I began to hum an old Rolling Stones song, because retro is always cool. In the distance a girl with long dark hair dashed out of a door at the far end of the building. She seemed to be headed in my general direction, so I looked away, pretending I hadn't seen her.

I climbed the one wide step and was reaching for the door when it flew open with a bang. A blur of green hair and combat boots whizzed past. Neither she nor the door actually touched me, but as I stepped back to get out of the way, I lost my balance and started to tip backward. I yanked my hands from my pockets and pinwheeled my arms wildly. In a last desperate move, I kicked one leg high trying to avoid the fall. To anyone watching through their high-powered binoculars, I'm sure I looked like the least talented member of an avant-garde dance troupe.

And it was all for nothing, because I fell anyway. I landed on the sidewalk flat on my butt, making a 100 percent unattractive smacking sound when I landed, like a pancake dropped from several feet onto a hard surface. Through sheer pianist's reflex, I had flung both my hands into the air to avoid injuring my fingers. My right shoe had come off during the miserable episode. And all I could wonder was *Who was THAT?* But I was too mortified to actually swing my head around and look for the green blur in combat boots.

"Moxie, my goodness! Are you hurt?" my mother cried.

I was, in fact, hurt. My butt was in a burning state of shock, and my ego felt bruised beyond repair. I had to crabwalk a few feet to retrieve my shoe and put it back on. I needed to immediately distance myself from this completely non-DUCK1 tumble, so I leaped to my feet, reached the door in one hop, yanked it open, and rushed through.

I stopped just inside the door of the dormitory to let my eyes adjust. Whereas outside, everything had been brilliantly hued, like a Hallmark version of reality, inside, everything was cool and dark and quiet. Like I imagined a funeral home might be. The floors were polished marble, and dark and elegantly paneled wood walls lined the hallway. Directly across from the entrance was an alcove that had been tastefully furnished with two delicately upholstered chairs and a small wooden table. The alcove looked like it was expecting Jane Austen and Louisa May Alcott for tea.

My parents were right behind me.

"Mox, are you all right?" my mother repeated. I refused to turn around and look her in the eye.

"Why wouldn't I be?" I asked. I had humiliated myself in plain view of the world, and I certainly didn't want to discuss it, or imagine how many people might have witnessed my charming dance rendition of *Spaz Lake*. I deferred further questioning by making my way down the hallway, resisting the impulse to rub both hands on my smarting backside.

The hallway opened into a larger alcove, where twin staircases spiraled upward on either side of the room.

Beneath the stairs a large doorway opened into Sage's living room, decorated with overstuffed couches and a small piano. It reminded me of Baron von Trapp's mansion in *The Sound of Music*. In the center of the alcove was a large oil painting of a remarkably plain woman wearing some kind of doily on her head. Her intense but humorless eyes followed the progress of the Kipper family toward the staircase. Everything smelled of wood polish.

We made our way up the giant staircase, which wrapped around to become a balcony that completely encircled the alcove below. I heard the sound of loud, thundering footsteps behind me. I instinctively moved to the right. Just in time. The green-haired, combat-boot-wearing blur shot past me. I saw only enough of her to note that she clutched a bronze object like a football, tucked neatly under one arm. She was followed closely by a dark-haired wisp of a girl in a peasant skirt who ran much more quietly, leaving a faint scent of patchouli in her wake. They rounded a second flight of stairs and disappeared.

"Wasn't that the same girl who knocked you down?" asked my father. "She didn't even apologize."

"She didn't knock me down, Dad," I said, acutely embarrassed. "She never even saw me. I accidentally backed off the step."

"I think it *was* the same girl," my mother said, in an outraged voice she usually reserved for Republicans. "What kind of manners does she have, charging past us like that? Was she raised in a barn?"

"Mom, please," I said. "There's no law against running up the stairs. And barns don't even *have* stairs."

I hoped no one could hear us. With all the embarrassing circumstances that had cropped up, I had completely forgotten to act Detached and Unique. Fortunately, we seemed to be the only people on the staircase. There wasn't another human being in sight.

At the far end of the balcony, a second, smaller staircase led to the third floor. I could hear the sounds of voices up there, which grew louder as I climbed the stairs, my parents trailing behind me. When I reached the top, I took a breath, then pushed open the glass double doors.

Into chaos.

There were parents and girls milling about—examining the hallway, standing in the doorways of rooms, dragging suitcases and boxes every which way. It was like there'd recently been a revolution, and a new regime of thirteen-year-olds was rapidly being installed in the capitol building. I tried to make Bold Eye Contact with several of the girls, but no one seemed to notice I was standing there.

"So this is where everyone is," my dad said. "I was beginning to wonder."

"The admissions letter said only new students come today. Everyone else arrives tomorrow," I told him.

"We didn't bring any of your stuff up," my mother said, looking around.

The thought of going back down all those stairs, past the doily lady, past the Mavix and the surreal lawn . . . I didn't think I could stand it. My butt was still killing me, and my ego still hurt too. Stairs should be avoided for as long as possible.

My mother must have read something in my face. I was afraid she was going to do something weird, like go in for the killer hug, or start singing to me. I love my mother, but she has a tendency to act in embarrassing ways when we're in public. And when we're alone. But I give her credit—she could sometimes tell when she was embarrassing me, and she didn't get all hurt about it. She touched my dad on the shoulder.

"Gil, let's you and I go get Moxie's stuff from the car, so she can meet her roommates and some of the other girls without us cramping her style."

The expression made me squirm. But when she was right, she was right. I didn't want to meet people I'd be living with all year standing next to a woman with terrier hair and a "Save the Tundra" T-shirt hiding the top half of a pair of mom jeans. And heaven forbid my father started in on his soda stories.

Before my parents were safely out of sight, a tall, athletic girl with a clipboard loped purposefully down the hall, her thick blond ponytail bouncing jauntily. She was clearly headed straight for us. Her stride was so powerful my first impulse was to duck and cover my head. But I refrained.

"Hey there!" she said loudly, grinning at us. "I'm Kristen, the proctor. You are . . . ?"

"The Kippers," my father said, sounding proud, as if he'd just won something. "Gil and Dallas, and this," he continued, relishing the *this*, "is Moxie."

I gave the proctor an impassive and, I hoped, unreadable stare. Then, when she least expected it, I shot my left eyebrow up.

"Fabulous to meet you—awesome!" Kristen said. She sounded like *she'd* just won something too. "Let's get you to your room. One of your roomies is already here. The other one isn't coming until later in the semester. So you'll have the triple to yourselves for a while."

"Moxie's dad and I are going to run downstairs and start bringing in her things," my mother said.

Yes. Thank you. Seriously.

Kristen nodded vigorously, her ponytail swishing up and down. I felt like if I watched it sway too long, I would sink into a deep, hypnotic sleep. Maybe that's how she controlled the new kids.

"Sounds good," Kristen said, making a note on her clipboard. What could the note say? *Student arrived at room without luggage, Student mesmerized by my ponytail, Student seems markedly nothing in particular.*

"There's a service elevator in the basement, which you can get to from the Sage parking lot—look for a red door near the fire lane. That's it," Kristen explained.

My mother discreetly squeezed my elbow.

"Alrightee then," she said. "Back in a jiffy."

More embarrassing language, but at this point I was willing to forgive.

My parents set out toward the double doors with the seriousness of Lewis and Clark embarking on their transcontinental exploration of North America. Kristen was watching me intently.

"They're coming back," I said, because she looked like she was waiting for me to drop into a sobbing heap at her feet.

Kristen continued to peer at me with intensity for a moment, then suddenly without warning she enfolded me in a terrifying hug.

"You're going to be just fiiiiiiiiiiiiiine," she said.

"I know that," I said, my voice muffled in her shoulder. It was obvious that my entire future as a cool person depended on my not crying at this moment. I quickly summoned the memory of the removal of a plantar wart from the sole of my foot in August. Picturing the injection of painkiller they shot right into that sucker jolted me from tears to disgust. Anything was better than tears right now. Even nausea.

Kristen smelled of freshly cut grass and Tiger Balm sports ointment. I think there was a whiff of field hockey stick in there too. After an awkward moment, I wiggled free of her hug. She continued to give me a wide-eyed, sympathetic smile.

"Okay, so this is your room, 303. One of the best triples—I had this room my freshman year. You've got great views of the quad, separate bedrooms, and two of you will have sinks."

Was that a status symbol here at Eaton? To have a sink?

Kristen pushed the door to 303 open while simultaneously making a little knocking sound with her knuckles. She glanced at her clipboard.

"Hello? Megan?"

There wasn't anyone I could see in the room we'd just walked into. It was large, with three tall windows, high ceilings, and a wood floor. Against the right wall was a bed, just a bare mattress and pillows. Against the left wall was a desk and a lamp. On both walls there were doors, and one of them opened.

"I told you I don't go by that name," came a voice.

Kristen checked her clipboard again, and made a little notation.

"Sorry," she said. "Spinky. Moxie Kipper, meet one of your roommates, Spinky Spanger."

When she emerged through the door, all I registered was green hair and combat boots. Zounds. What were the chances? Had she seen me fall smack onto my can? I tried to keep my face totally blank.

Spinky Spanger walked to the center of the room and appraised me with a frank look. I tried to raise my eyebrow at her, but it was temporarily paralyzed.

Spinky was dressed in black jeans, the aforementioned combat boots, and a ripped T-shirt that had been modified by the strategic placement of safety pins. She had something around her neck that resembled, or possibly was, a dog's chain collar. Her hair, short and standing straight up in a classic brush cut, wasn't just green. It was an aggressive, leaking radiation shade of green. Earrings adorned all available real estate on her left earlobe, from fleshy bottom to rounded top. A tiny silver hoop hung through one eyebrow. Her nails were painted indigo blue, and most of them were chipped. She continued to stare at me frankly, hands on hips, like I was a horse she was considering buying.

Kristen looked back and forth between the two of us. I could tell right off that Spinky confused Kristen. I liked that. I wanted to confuse Kristen too. Possibly even worry her.

"Well, I could leave you two to get to know each other," Kristen said, but she addressed it to me almost as if it were a question.

"Yeah," I said, nodding.

She hesitated for a fraction of a second. So I sat down on the bed and propped my feet up, to show Kristen I felt at home. She turned to go, and I watched the last of her blond locks whip around the door frame. Then everything was silent.

I was alone with Spinky Spanger.

CHapter Three

"**M**oxie," Spinky said thoughtfully, like she was trying to get the feel of it on her tongue. "Moxie."

I just sat there on the bed, because I hadn't decided how to respond. Which was nothing new. My intuition told me my best bet was to stick with my DUCKI personality in this girl's company. But Spinky appeared so detached and coolly unique herself, I figured I'd better ramp it up a notch. I could already tell that this was a person I wanted to impress.

"It's a . . . there's this soda and two presidents . . . I mean, I'm supposed to be . . ."

Spinky waited patiently for my mouth and my brain to coordinate. *Speak*, I commanded myself.

"My parents really should have gone to Remedial Child-Naming School," I finally forced out. Okay, deep breath. "My theory is if you're going to go for a weird name, go the whole hog, like Frank Zappa. He named his kids Moon Unit and Dweezil."

Spinky regarded me thoughtfully. I tried to hide my amazement that I had said something aloud in a complete sentence.

"Are you a Frank Zappa fan?" she asked.

Oh. I had no idea. This saying things out loud thing was tricky. I'd only picked up that tidbit after my father watched a documentary on Zappa and spent the next two days randomly declaring, "Moon Unit! Dweezil! Have you ever heard such crazy names?" And frankly, yes I *had*.

But wait. It was my turn to talk again. I needed to say something unexpected.

"I'm not a fan of *fans*," I said cryptically, pursing my lips. "It's like Rimbaud said—worship is for the masses."

Now *that* I had simply made up. There was a Rimbaud, I was pretty sure. He was . . . wait, a French playwright? Poet? Designer? My mother had been talking about him at breakfast, but only his name had penetrated my psyche. I was banking on the fact that he was obscure enough that he very well *could* have said "Worship is for the masses," no matter what his profession.

Spinky let out a deep chuckle. I prayed to the gods of Cool Detachment that she was laughing with me, not at me.

I examined her boots to avoid making eye contact. They were well worn and laced up tightly, her black jeans tucked perfectly inside with no billowing bubble-over. I raised my gaze slightly to one of her hands. She had a silver ring on every finger, including her thumb. One of the rings was fashioned in the shape of a skull. A leather thong was wrapped around her wrist, and my eyes widened as I caught sight of a series of squiggles and lines on her forearm.

Spinky Spanger had a *tattoo*.

I immediately wanted one.

"Nice tat," I said, gesturing toward her arm. "I've been wanting to get one, but the thought of peeling Gil and Dallas off the ceiling has slowed me down."

"Really—you're thinking of getting some ink? Like what?" Spinky asked.

I trolled the depths of my mind to come up with something simultaneously weird and edgy.

"A cockroach," I blurted. "To . . . you know. Defy the limits of cultural acceptability."

Spinky looked delighted.

"Excellent! Tell me when you decide to do it—I want to go with you!"

I nodded enthusiastically while praying Spinky suffered from short-term memory loss.

"So this is all kind of weird," I said, redirecting the subject.

"The room?" Spinky asked.

"Boarding school," I said.

Spinky slid one of her rings off and started to play with it.

"You didn't want to come to Eaton?" she asked.

"Well," I said, heaving a sigh, "I didn't have much choice. It was boarding school or six months of community service."

Spinky arched one eyebrow, which bummed me out. I was sort of hoping to corner the market on eyebrow raising.

"Community service? Did you get busted for something?"

I looked around the room like I was checking for eavesdroppers or microphones. Then I dropped my voice to a whisper.

"My lawyer said I'm not supposed to talk about it," I murmured. Just then my stomach growled.

Spinky looked at me intently, then slid the ring back onto her finger. "Gotcha," she said.

YES! There's nothing to cement a potentially DUCKI personality than the hint of a criminal background. I felt my face flush with accomplishment. You know, I might actually be good at this potential personality thing. Maybe one day I could even do it, like, for a *living*.

"Well, I'm here to honor tradition," Spinky told me. "Half the women in my family have gone here, going back a hundred years. Three generations of them are already in love with this place. But I'm the first one not to get a dorm room in Williams House—I guess it's only upperclassmen now."

"Guess you'll have to settle for the Sage Institute for the Criminally Insane," I mumbled.

Spinky burst out laughing. The grin transformed her face into something almost sweet, despite the green hair. She looked like a cheerful leprechaun.

"Sage Institute for the Criminally Insane," Spinky repeated. "You crack me up, Moxie from Biloxi."

I blushed with relief. I'd made her laugh—and I hadn't even meant to. Score one for the DUCKI.

"I'm from Pine Point, actually," I said. "Not Biloxi."

That was a stupid thing to say. Who cared where I lived, anyway?

"I'm just rhyming," Spinky said. "Old habit—I'm told

people get used to it. Keeps me on my toes for writing poetry."

Spinky Spanger wrote poetry? This didn't mesh with her Rebel image. But then again there was poetry, and there was *poetry*. I suspected the poetry of Spinky Spanger, if published, would be banned in most states.

"Cool," I said.

I looked around the room, trying to come up with something else Detached and Unique to talk about.

"You should pounce on the other single," Spinky said, gesturing toward the door on the left. "The person who lives in the middle room will have to deal with people schlepping in and out all the time. No privacy. And I sing in my sleep," she added cryptically.

"Okay," I agreed. I walked over and peered inside. The room was small, simple, and cozy. There was a closet, a dresser, a desk, and a bed, with a beige blanket folded neatly at its foot. The famous sink gleamed white in the corner. A large window squared a view of the impossibly green lawn of inner campus.

"So Mox, what do you say we—"

"Hello, hello!"

Zounds. Spinky's question was interrupted by the abominably timed return of Gil and Dallas Kipper.

I turned to see my mother framed in the doorway, holding a huge suitcase. My father was behind her. They were both staring at Spinky like they were fairly certain they'd just seen her photo on *America's Most Wanted*. I saw my mother's gaze fall on Spinky's eyebrow ring with a little scowl. Then I saw her gaze drop to the tattoo. The scowl deepened. There was, what they call in the theatre, a pregnant pause.

"Mom, Dad, this is my roommate, Spinky. Spinky, meet Gil and Dallas," I said. It came out more like a command than simple good manners.

I made eye contact with Spinky, furrowing my brow in an attempt to convey to her that I was not responsible for the many possible shortcomings of these two middle-aged humans.

"Yes, actually, I think you knocked my—"

I cut my mother off abruptly.

"My room's in here—come see!"

My mother hesitated, still frowning at Spinky. If I knew Dallas Kipper, and believe me I did, she was thinking about taking Spinky to task for charging around like a linebacker, causing innocent people to experience injuries to the posterior region. Not to mention a lecture on the evils of piercing and permanent body art. I walked across the room as fast as I could without sprinting, grabbed my mother's hand, and physically hauled her across the floor and into my little single.

"See, what'd I tell you, isn't it adorable?" I said very loudly. I was concerned that I'd left Gil Kipper in the main room with Spinky. But I knew Gil Kipper too, and dollars to donuts he wasn't going to say anything at all. He'd simply adjust his watch band and smooth his shirt into place and clear his throat multiple times. It's just his way.

"I'm a little concerned," my mother whispered, "about the situation. I'm not sure Spinky is the best roommate for you."

Uh-oh. Whenever my mother said she was "concerned," it was cause for serious alarm. After a mere running-in-a-walking-zone infraction and a few unconventional personal style choices, my mother had decided Spinky was a Bad Influence. I didn't have the time or the patience to convince her that Spinky was the best roommate I could have dreamed of. Dallas would never buy it. And with her activism experience, it was quite possible she might march directly to the dean's office and demand a room switch.

I had to get my parents out of here!

"So, thanks," I said, looking at my shoes. "I can, you know. Take it from here."

"Mox, I'm not comfortable—"

"Mom!" I whispered. "I. Am. Fine."

She narrowed her eyes at me. Clearly she was not going gently into that good night.

"Plus, wow, is it almost three already? There's that required thing I need to get to—I'll just throw my bags in my room. Seriously, Mom. You guys should take off because I've got to get to this thing. We all do."

"What thing?" she asked. I had her by the arm and was leading her out the door.

"It's right there in the schedule—the important . . . It has to do with . . ." Oh, what was the word I needed? What was it?

"Orientation?" my mother asked.

"Exactly!" I cried. "Yes. Gotta get to Educational Enrichment orientation—cannot miss that. So important. And I'm already late."

Now all four of us were standing in the center room. My father was checking his watch and adjusting his glasses. Spinky was watching me and my mother with a small smile on her face.

"I'll call you tonight," I said.

My father, never comfortable with situations that involved a) possibly emotional good-byes, or b) proximity to a green-haired teenage girl, spoke up.

"Well then, we better get going. Mox, take care of yourself."

He gave me his signature hug-noogie hybrid, rubbing the top of my head with his knuckles.

"Bye Dad."

I gave my mother a hug. When I felt tears in my eyes, I thought about my plantar wart again.

"Bye, Mom."

Okay. I was making progress. Hugs and good-byes had been exchanged.

"Drive safely," I added, because it looked like they needed a touch more help getting out of the room.

I was getting ready to put my hand on my mother's back and physically usher her into the hallway when my dad suddenly took her hand and started leading her out.

"Okay then, Mox. Call if you need anything, anything at all," he said.

"Bye, honey," my mother said from the doorway.

I waved. I felt bad to have basically ejected them from my room, but I had clearly ended up with the coolest new kid in school as my roommate, and I couldn't let my mother turn it into a federal case.

When they were safely out of sight, I made an explosive sound of irritation. Spinky looked thoughtful.

"They didn't seem that bad. Well, your mom was a little

tense, maybe. Hey, do the tuna need to be saved? I thought it was the dolphins."

I sighed.

"It said Save the *Tundra*," I told her wearily.

Spinky's expression told me that explained a great deal.

"She didn't like me. That's for sure."

I stared at Spinky in alarm, thinking fast.

"It's actually because . . . you . . . look a lot like this other girl who was . . . you know. I'm not really supposed to talk about it—but this other girl who kind of . . . also had to choose between community service and boarding school."

"Ah, the Bad Influence," Spinky said, grinning.

"Yeah. Anyway, she chose community service. And my mother kind of has a . . . thing about her."

"Righteous. Doesn't bother me, Mox." Spinky waved her hand like she was swatting away a fly. "I stopped worrying about that stuff a long time ago. But speaking of parents, I gotta go Graham Bell the Aged Ps."

I hesitated. What? My stomach started rumbling again.

Spinky gave me a leprechaun grin.

"I gotta go call my parents. I actually flew out of Oregon last night, and I was supposed to check in with them first thing this morning. They get anxious."

I nodded, a little relieved Spinky was leaving. It was a lot harder than I'd thought to maintain the DUCKI personality for more than a few minutes at a time. It wasn't just coming up with stuff to say, but actually saying it out loud that was tricky. But so far, I felt like I'd done okay after a few false starts. I felt pretty confident that to Spinky, I appeared to be an edgy, cool, detached, and possibly criminal person— minus my current outfit of Dockers and a faded pink T-shirt that said "I Love Tofu." Hopefully, she'd decided that I was a worthy roommate for her, that Moxie Roosevelt Kipper was Trouble.

Spinky walked out into the hallway, then stuck her head back in the door.

"I forgot to ask. How's your butt?"

Zounds.

Chapter Four

I hadn't invented the "required thing" I'd used to ward off my parents. There really was something on the schedule from 3:00 to 4:00—new students' Educational Enrichment signup, conveniently located on the ground level in Sage Living Room.

During my admissions interview, I'd been told in great detail about the Educational Enrichment program, usually just called EE. Eaton was very proud of its unique EE, and offered choices ranging from yoga to public speaking, with a wide variety of strange options in between. I had thought that maybe with the special course of study I had planned with Mr. Tate for piano, that I'd be exempt. My admissions packet had indicated I was not to be so lucky. It was crucial that I make an EE choice that could work with any number of possible personalities. I didn't want to end up deciding on Detached, Unique, Coolly Knowing Individual when I'd signed up for Square Dancing. Or going for Mysterious Earth Goddess, for example, when I'd signed up for Young Capitalists. You see my point.

I would have preferred to go to signup with Spinky along as my armor, but it was already 3:30. For all I knew, she had already been to signup. I left my room quickly, passing a waif of a girl with dark silky hair and spacey eyes who smelled like patchouli and who was also heading for the stairs.

I found the entrance to Sage Living Room between the twin staircases that faced the painting of the somber doily-faced lady I was beginning to think of as Auntie Sparkles. There was already a group of girls there, standing by long tables containing sheets of information and clipboards. I resisted the impulse to rush to the tables. I made myself saunter instead, and it seemed to take twenty minutes for my casual amble to transport me to the nearest EE information sheet and signup clipboard. I was momentarily paralyzed by choices.

The first one I saw was called The Tao of Dance.

Definitely no. Dancing did not enter into any of my potential personalities; it only lingered in their collective nightmares. Next was Faith: the Individual Pursuit and World Religions. That actually sounded kind of interesting, but I couldn't think how it would relate to me personally. That is, any of my personalities. I moved on. Green You: Living Harmoniously with the Planet. I made a note of its location—table two, clipboard farthest to the right. That one might work. There was enough latitude to fit DUCKI, MEG, and definitely Assertive Revolutionary Activist. I worried a lot about the state of the planet, especially the things living on it. I once planned to sneak into a fish shop and liberate all the lobsters they kept in the tank. Maybe I could resurrect that dream in Green You.

The next selection was Self-Confidence Through Comedy: Release Your Inner Stand-Up. Yikes. That sounded pathetic.

As I moved farther down the tables, none of the subjects seemed like good candidates. Cooking. Chess. History of music—definitely not. I was trying to escape the boring old Moxie, not reinforce my doofus-level knowledge of composers. Poetry. Poetry? Was it possible Spinky would take that one? Knowing what EE my roommate would want would be a huge help. But so far, I hadn't caught a glimpse of her lawn-topped head.

I got a sudden whiff of patchouli, and turned to find the silky-haired girl I'd seen back on the hallway. Her eyes were very wide, and an unusually pale shade of blue.

"Hey," she said. "Didn't I see you back on Sage 3?"

I nodded. I felt like I might have run into her before that. Had she been behind me at the Mavix's registration table?

"Room 303," I said. "I'm Spinky's roommate," I added, then instantly regretted my gooberish self-important tone.

"305," she said. "My name's Haven. Your roommate is excellent. She tried to help me rig up an incense burner outside my window. Lighting it up inside is an expellable offense, apparently. It wouldn't stay put because the brass base is pretty heavy, but she said she was going to find some duct tape and a counterweight to strap it down. Cool girl."

That's why she looked familiar. She was the owner of the mysterious plummeting object.

"Spinky's great," I affirmed.

"What's the story with your missing roommate?" Haven asked. "I heard she started last year, then she set something on fire in bio and got sent home."

"Wow, I have no idea," I said. Set something on fire?

"Maybe she's just cycling into her fire era," Haven mused. "She'll be back when she transitions over to air or water."

I nodded, like I had just been about to say the exact same thing myself.

Haven had baby-fine hair parted in the center that hung around her face. She was wearing a tank top decorated with a faded Buddha, and a gauzy peasant skirt. Completing the picture were feather earrings and a silver necklace from which hung a square pendant. She moved like she was underwater, slow and easy and languid. Her lips seemed to naturally reside in a small, peaceful smile. I got the feeling that firecrackers could go off right next to Haven, and she wouldn't be especially startled.

Without thinking about it, I adapted my movements to hers. It felt nice to step into that sleepy, graceful posture.

"I'm Moxie," I said. "I guess we're next-door neighbors."

"Cool," Haven said.

My eye was drawn back to the pendant around her neck. It held a picture of an older man with glasses and a crew cut, wearing a maroon robe and the merriest smile I'd ever seen.

"Is that your dad?" I asked.

Haven laughed, but it was a sweet laugh, like little bells.

"That's the Dalai Lama," she said. "He's kind of like my guru. So I guess he is my dad, spiritually speaking."

I'd never met anyone who had a guru. Actually, I wasn't precisely sure what a guru was, but it sounded exotic and

46

enticing, and I immediately wanted one too. There was something soothing about Haven that appealed to me. She certainly didn't look like she gave a second's thought to what anyone might think of her.

"The vibration is nice in here," Haven remarked, tucking her hair behind an ear. "High and bright, you know?"

I nodded thoughtfully, while wondering what Haven meant. Nothing was registering on my personal Richter scale. What exactly was a vibration? Just say something, I commanded myself.

"Definitely nice vibration—thank the goddess!" I declared. I'd heard that on a rerun of *Xena: Warrior Princess*, but it sounded good. And anyway, Haven could potentially qualify as a goddess herself, so I was just sort of being polite.

"Goddess worshipper, huh?" Haven said, her lips curving in a fetching half smile. "That's cool. I've always dug Wicca."

I was unable to translate Haven's remarks into Moxie-Speak. So I changed the subject, because I wanted her to keep talking to me.

"What are you going to sign up for?" I asked.

"Already done," Haven said. "I signed up for Green You when I came in." She gestured toward one of the EF tables.

"That's what I want to sign up for," I exclaimed.

"Better hurry. It was already filling up when I got the clipboard."

I abandoned Haven in a rush, and edged and squirmed my way up to the table I remembered having the Green You signup sheet. A hefty girl dressed in denim from neck to ankle edged in front of me. I scowled. Was she trying to ruin my life?

Denim Girl hoisted a clipboard in the air and bellowed across the room.

"Tiff! Tiffany! Are you signing up for Green You? It'll fill up if you wait!"

Opportunity! In what I admit was an incredibly obnoxious move, I reached up and grabbed the clipboard from Denim Girl. The first page of Green You must have already filled up, because a new one had been added. I hastily signed my name, hoping it wasn't too late, and handed the clipboard back to Denim Girl before ducking out of the crowd. Haven was waiting by the living room double doors. I squirmed past people and headed over to her.

"Did you get it?" Haven asked.

I nodded triumphantly.

"Someone had the clipboard right there, like they were saving it for me. I seriously think it was a legitimate instance of Divine Intervention!"

Haven laughed.

"Good for you, Wicca," she said.

Had Haven just called me Wicca? A MEG nickname! A thrill shot straight through my toes and down into the heart of Mother Earth. I was legit. But I better get straight to a dictionary and look it up, so I could behave accordingly. I would be serene, organic, transcendental, and vegetarian. I would listen to the Beatles and watch Woodstock documentaries. I would wear peasant blouses and Indian-print skirts, and perhaps learn to weave in my spare time. I could get a poster of Jimi Hendrix for my room . . .

My room. Where Spinky lived. In my room, I was a DUCKI. If I was going to successfully try out my personalities, I needed to keep track of them. I pressed my hands over my stomach, where a trill of nervous energy fluttered. I would have to keep a list—a Personality Log, where I would write down details for easy reference, so I would not accidentally mention wanting tofurkey for Thanksgiving to Spinky, or asking Haven where to shop for combat boots. As long as I kept everything straight, the Moxie Personality Experiment could continue full blast.

"Should we go back up to Sage 3?" I asked.

Haven nodded. "I'm not really into crowds," she said.

"The worst," I agreed.

The din from Sage Living Room faded abruptly when we reached the foyer. Auntie Sparkles gazed gravely down at me from her frame. I flashed her a wide grin. I couldn't help it—I felt so happy. Being a MEG felt great—it was definitely a top contender alongside DUCKI. Haven was amazing. *And* I'd signed up for Green You!

Life was good.

Kristen was standing in the center of the Sage 3 hall when we got there, like a gatekeeper. I wouldn't have been all too surprised if she had intoned "NONE SHALL PASS." But instead she waved Haven over.

"Haven, your roommate got in while you were downstairs," Kristen said. "Want to come meet her?"

"Cool," Haven said, nodding. "Catch you later, Wicca."

"Later," I said, shooting Kristen a glance to make sure she'd noticed what Haven had called me. I mean, how cool was I that someone with a guru was already my friend?

I don't think Kristen noticed.

Still smiling, I went into our room, looking forward to seeing Spinky.

But the scowling person standing in the middle of the floor with her arms folded over her chest was most assuredly *not* Spinky Spanger.

Chapter Five

"**Oh**, hi," I said. My inner MEG fizzled. Nor did my DUCKI rear its feathered head. I proceeded with caution. "Do you live on this hall?"

She shook her head, and my memory rippled. I felt I knew her from somewhere.

"Kate," she said, pointing to herself. "I'm waiting for Spinky."

Her clothes were nondescript. Short-sleeved shirt and jeans. No visible jewelry. She was a bit pale, with reddish blond hair pulled back in a high ponytail. Her features were a little pinched, like maybe her face had gotten a bit thinner than it meant to. She was neither Jock nor Rebel nor Hipper Than Thou—I wasn't sure what to make of her. Unless hostile was a valid personality type.

"I'm Moxie Kipper," I said, trying to remain expressionless. "So, you know Spinky?"

"Yeah," Kate said, looking over my shoulder at the doorway. "From before."

I opened my mouth to say something that would stake my claim as Spinky's best and oldest friend at Eaton. But nothing came out. I couldn't figure out this Kate person. How was I supposed to know the right thing to say to her?

We stood there, facing each other, like a couple of bookends. Kate was apparently not the sort of person who felt the need to make small talk. I, on the other hand, was. Desperately.

"So, do you live on one of the other Sage halls?" I asked in a cheerful voice. Cripes. I sounded like Dallas Kipper.

"Yeah," Kate replied. "Sage 3 Long."

Sage third floor was divided into three separate halls: Sage 3 Short, where I lived, Sage 3 Long, and Sage Zoo, which was mostly seniors.

"Um, did you by any chance go to Camp Migawam?" I asked, trying not to study her face too obviously.

Kate looked at me like I was a bug.

"No."

I felt my face turn red, and a flash of irritation rose in my chest. Was it such an absurd question? What was her problem? This was *my* room after all. I decided to play the Spinky card.

"Well, have a seat, make yourself at home. Spinky could be back in ten minutes or five hours. You know how she can be!" I forced a laugh.

Kate took a seat on the spare bed.

"Yeah, I know how she can be," Kate said. And she actually gave me a tiny smile. The lowest possible degree of one, but the corners of her lips turned up microscopically. Encouraged, I plunged ahead.

"Yeah, I love Spinky. Talk about lucking out in the roommate department. She's the best."

"My roommate is an idiot," Kate told me. "Gucci this and Prada that. Christian LeBoutin shoes, blah blah blah. Her motto is apparently 'Get the most expensive one.' She plays classical music all the time like she's just so highbrow. Please. I have no use for her whatsoever. Spinky Spanger— now *she* is real people."

I tried not to frown over the classical music remark as Kate paused for a breath. Most of the CDs I had brought with me were classical. It hadn't occurred to me that my personality modification should be extended to my music collection. But at least I could now define one thing about Kate's personality—she disliked the wealthy. I nodded, thought of something to say, and chimed in.

"Do her parents drive a Hummer? I hate those things. There's just no excuse to drive something that big and gas-guzzling," I said, a little loudly. I was raised to hate all supersized personal motor vehicles, with a particular venom reserved especially for Hummers. My mother once reached into her reusable shopping bag and hurled a loaf of organic eight-grain bread at an unoccupied Hummer that was parked in a handicapped spot at the Shop & Save.

"Whatever," Kate said. "I come from a family of cops. My dad is a cop. My two uncles are cops. My oldest brother is at the academy. This tiara-girl stuff is all new to me. Spinky's no tiara-girl."

"Oh god, no," I said, laughing. "And neither am I."

Kate looked at me, but she didn't say anything. I got the feeling she hadn't made up her mind *what* I was. Well, that made two of us.

"I'm here on scholarship," I added. I deleted the detail that the scholarship was of the musical, "highbrow" variety.

Her expression softened.

"Oh, yeah, okay. Yeah—me too."

Another long pause.

"So how's your hall? Do you like the people?" I asked.

I sounded like I was hosting my own morning show, but the thought of sitting alone in my room with someone and not talking to them was like going to an all you can eat dessert buffet and not getting anything.

"Not really," Kate said, looking glum. "It seems like all the trust fund babies ended up on 3 Long. They're all richies."

"All of them?"

Kate shrugged. "I don't know. Most of them. The ones I've met."

"I've only met one of my hallmates, but she's definitely not a trust fund baby. She's really spiritual. She has a guru!"

"That's messed up," Kate said.

"Oh, not at all," I said. "No, she's really cool."

"Sounds a little culty," Kate said, glancing at her watch. "Like that Scientology stuff."

"Oh, no," I said. "I don't think it's like that."

Kate shrugged. I was ready to jump right back in and defend Haven's honor, but Kate seemed to have lost interest in the subject. Another uncomfortable silence followed.

"Have you ever been to Pine Point? I'm just wondering if maybe we've ever run into each other somewhere. Piano lessons or something?"

Gah! I forgot I wasn't supposed to mention my square-headed music habit.

Kate stood up.

"I'm tone-deaf," she said. "I need to get going. Can you just tell Spinky I stopped by?"

I stood up too. Did she really have to go, or was she irritated with me? I had no clue how to figure this girl out. Nor would I want to, except for the fact that she and Spinky were apparently friends.

"I'll definitely tell her. Kate . . . what did you say your last name was?"

Kate stopped in the doorway and looked back at me.

"Southington," she said, after a second. Then she scowled a little.

"I'll tell her," I said.

Kate disappeared without thanking me.

Spinky remained missing until dinner, when we were joyfully reunited at the bread and salad bar. I noticed people looking at her, and I puffed up a little to find myself casually chatting with the tough-looking girl who wore a dog collar as a necklace. I followed her to a table where she had been sitting alone with a wide variety of beverages and several different bowls of partially eaten cereal surrounding the remains of her entrée. She had already finished most of her dinner, so I created a quickie meal of placebo salads—potato, macaroni, and pasta—that have very little by way of green leafy matter and are definitely not diet items, but still fall under the generous "salad" umbrella.

"I'm almost done," I said, my mouth partially full. Our table was close to the double doors, which opened onto Auntie Sparkles's foyer and faced the Sage Living Room, and I had noticed Spinky casting glances at the exit, like she was eager to get going.

"No hurry," Spinky said. "But they're supposed to post the EE lists on the hall bulletin board during dinner, and I want to make sure I got into Green You. I was the first one to sign up, so I don't think it'll be a problem."

"That's so funny, I signed up for that too, and so did someone else from our hall," I said. "Haven—I think you already know her, right?"

"Haven the Buddhist," Spinky said. "She's awesome."

"Isn't she totally? Well anyway, there was a rush on the signup sheets by the time I got there. I was so scared I'd get stuck in the Tao of Dance," I declared, and added a relieved chuckle.

"Really? I thought that one sounded good," Spinky said, plucking a piece of pasta salad off my plate and popping it into her mouth with her fingers.

"Oh. I'm just not very good on my feet," I said, recovering fast. I was confused. What could be less DUCKI than the Tao of Dance? And yet Spinky was undeniably the poster girl of DUCKIs. "Hey listen, a girl stopped by to see you this afternoon," I said, changing the subject. "A friend of yours from back home or something? Name was Kate."

Spinky looked at me blankly.

"Strawberry blond hair? On the tall side? Kind of bony?"

"And she said she was from Oregon?" Spinky asked, looking genuinely confused.

"Well, no, not exactly. She said she knew you from before. Oh, Southington. That was her last name. Kate Southington."

Spinky's face remained blank. Then her eyebrows shot up in tandem.

"Okay, I remember now. I *have* met her before—at an incoming new students reception last year. I was on campus because it was my mother's thirtieth Eaton reunion. We hung out a little."

So they weren't besties from back home. I felt a happy tide of relief. I started to ask another question, but Spinky interrupted me.

"No rush, but are you done eating yet?"

For Spinky, anything.

"I'm done," I said.

We bused our trays and headed through the foyer. Without thinking, I gave the big oil painting a cheerful wave.

"See somebody you know?" Spinky said, glancing back in the direction I'd waved.

I blushed. This was one of those times when honesty seemed like the best policy, be it DUCKI or not.

"I was waving at Auntie Sparkles," I admitted, pointing to the painting of the dour, doily-headed woman.

Spinky looked from the painting to me, and burst out laughing.

"Oh my gosh, that is hysterical! I'm with you, Mox. From now on Amelia Eaton is officially Auntie Sparkles."

We trudged up the stairs still laughing. I suppose somewhere Amelia Eaton was turning over in her grave, but what the heck. I'd made Spinky Spanger laugh.

When we reached our hall, we were just in time to see Kristen tacking a paper to the bulletin board.

"Bet that's it," Spinky said. She linked her arm in mine, and we walked over to the bulletin board as Kristen retreated down the hall.

The list was typed in alphabetical order.

"Yay, Green You! I'm in," Spinky said. "Where are you—

Oh my god, I've forgotten your last name! I've got new student dementia. Didn't you say you signed up for Green You, Mox?"

I was staring at the list, my mind suddenly blank. Actually, not blank. No. Filled with panic, confusion, and horror. Because I *did* see my name.

I had been enrolled in Self-Confidence Through Comedy: Releasing Your Inner Stand-Up.

"It's a mistake," I said.

Spinky was running her finger down the list.

"There you are. The only Moxie at Eaton, I'll bet. Self-Confidence Through Comedy?"

"It's a horrible mistake. What am I going to do? It's a nightmare!"

Spinky turned her round, cheerful face toward me. She was wearing earrings shaped like little televisions and one of them was falling out.

"I think it's great for you, Mox. I think it's perfect."

Perfect? I reached over and fixed Spinky's earring. Perfect because I seemed to need self-confidence?

Spinky turned and headed for our room. I followed after her limply.

"They're going to have to let me switch to Green You," I said as we walked in. "I will fight the administration if I have to."

Spinky had stopped in the middle of the floor. "Do we need curtains for this center room?" she asked.

"I mean, they have to let me, right? They can't just do that to me. It's their mistake—a clerical error."

Spinky turned around and looked at me like she was surprised I was still behind her.

"Do what to you?" she asked. She lifted her shirt while she stood there and scratched her ribs with two blue fingernails, revealing a pleasantly rounded Buddha belly.

"Make me be in an EE I didn't sign up for and humiliate me!"

Spinky scratched a bit more, then shrugged.

"If you want to change, just ask the teacher assigned to your EE during orientation," Spinky said. "The worst that can happen is she'll say no. But I don't get why you would feel humiliated."

"Because of the class!" I declared. "Self-Confidence Through Comedy?"

Spinky waited for more.

"Release your Inner Stand-Up?" I threw up my hands. "It's ridiculous. I mean, the whole idea is so pathetic."

Spinky spied something on the window ledge and grabbed it. It was a roll of duct tape.

"There it is! I promised Haven I'd rig a sling and weight

for her incense burner with this. Don't worry too much, Mox. It's not as bad as you think."

Spinky was out the door without another word. Had I not already heard Haven telling me about Spinky's plans for the incense burner, I would have been certain my roommate was blowing me off with a very bizarre excuse.

I wandered into my room, found my sheets and comforter in one of my boxes, and made my bed. Now I had to lie in it.

It wasn't until I pulled my soft comforter up under my chin that I realized how exhausted I actually was.

I was well on my way into a deep sleep when, like a dream, Kate Southington's face flashed in my mind's eye. And this time I was absolutely sure that I knew her.

Before I had a chance to figure out how, I was fast asleep.

Chapter Six

My first meeting with Mr. Tate was the next morning, and I got to his office ten minutes early. Miss Nimetz, my Pine Point piano teacher for the last four years, was a great musician but sort of stodgy and grim. Mr. Tate had seemed, during our admissions meeting, to have tumbled out of a Southern novel filled with eccentric and unintentionally hilarious characters. I was fervently hoping that my first impression of him was correct, and that my piano lessons were about to get a lot more lively.

I sat down to wait for him on a wooden bench outside his office, and absentmindedly practiced fingering my scales using my algebra textbook as a keyboard. It seemed more useful than actually opening it, which had been my original, uncharacteristically ambitious plan.

Mr. Tate arrived precisely at 9:00 a.m., striding down the hall in a green mock turtleneck sweater, perfectly pressed jeans, and a pair of white Converse high-tops. His face was creased, his hair wild and silver, and his eyes a lively blue. He had the thickest and whitest eyebrows I'd ever seen.

"Moxie Roosevelt Kippah," he said in a deep, rumbly voice liberally tinged with a Southern accent. "Good aftahnoon. No, wait a minute."

He checked his watch.

"Pahdon me. Good mawnin'."

"Good morning," I replied, unable to stop myself from breaking into a huge smile. One lock of his hair was standing straight up on his head, like an exclamation mark.

Mr. Tate unlocked his office door and ushered me in. Most of the room was taken up by a baby grand piano. By the window was a small desk in front of a bookshelf crammed with music and books. The office was like Mr. Tate himself, partly tidy, partly all over the place.

He sat down behind his desk and indicated a wooden chair with a nod of his head.

"Take a seat, Miss Kippah. It's not very comfortable, I'm afraid, but some people have a tendency to fall asleep when

I talk to them, and I've got to fight back where I can."

I already knew that nothing in the world could make me fall asleep while Mr. Tate was talking. The chair *was* hard, though.

"Settlin' in, are you?" he asked, and I nodded.

"Really well, thanks," I replied.

"Well, good. I am very glad to have you here."

He pronounced the last word in two syllables—"heah."

"Would you like to start us off, Miss Kippah?"

"Start us off?"

"Play something,"

Duh. Of course that's what he meant.

I took a seat at the piano, played a few scales, then launched directly into the opening of the Goldberg Variations. I lost my self-consciousness within a few lines, then lost sight of the room, and eventually lost sight Mr. Tate himself, as Bach temporarily eclipsed my world. I played straight through the first ten variations, skipping only number 3, since it tripped me up a little sometimes. I wanted to be perfect for Mr. Tate in our first session.

I glanced over at him when I finished, trying not to look too eager. If he'd noticed my skipping Variation 3—and I'm sure he had—he didn't point it out. Instead, he sat back in his chair and put his hands on his knees.

Then he looked at me, both eyebrows drawn together in a tufty white V.

"You are a gifted pianist, Miss Kippah, but"—he paused—"more than that, you have music in your bones."

I felt my heart unclench and the blood rush happily into my face.

"I can always tell right away which ones are being pushed by their folks," he continued, "and which ones are doing it because the music is who they are. It comes through in every note you play, young lady, and that is the difference between an amateur and the real thing. You are the real thing. But you know that already."

Wow. Miss Nimetz forked out maybe one or two compliments in a year. I could get used to this.

"Well, I know I still have a lot of work to do," I said modestly, trying to eat my smile.

"Hope that you always will," he replied, running a hand through his hair, which produced an effect like a silver Mohawk. "When the day comes that you don't think you have any more work to do, when you think you're good enough and you've learned it all and you've become the pianist you intend to be for the rest of your life, that is the day you ought to stop playing. Do you enjoy Wilhelm Kempff?"

"Oh, yes, definitely," I said. "He's one of my favorite pianists—I have every single recording of his Beethoven sonatas."

"Yes, I understand they've put them on those little coaster-shaped things now."

"CDs," I said helpfully.

"That's right. I prefer records myself. Now, if you listen carefully, and follow along in a score, you can hear a mistake every now and again. And I'm sure you know that Kempff played into his eighties—with arthritis—and he made more mistakes then. Ones he didn't make as a younger man. And I'll tell you, Miss Kippah, I would rather hear Wilhelm Kempff's mistakes than I would most people's note-perfect renditions. Because he plays from the soul. And the soul of an artist is far more important than some silly notion of perfection."

I knew exactly what he meant. I had just never heard anyone express it so perfectly before.

"And that brings us back to you. Your Goldberg Variations are very solid. You understand Bach—you can transcend the math and logic of his music and communicate the *feeling* in it. Have you worked on all thirty of the variations?

"Yes," I said. "I mean, mostly. I've worked to some extent on all of them. Well, except for Variation 28."

"Ah, yes. The iceberg to the *Titanic* of many a hopeful virtuoso. Why haven't you tackled Variation 28?"

I hesitated. Mr. Tate's eyes gleamed as he sat back in his chair, folded his hands neatly over his stomach, and waited for my response.

"I guess I think . . . I don't know. I guess I just think it's for a more advanced student."

"And you're not an advanced student?" he asked.

"I . . . well, yes, I am. But I also think it's okay to know that there are some things that are still out of my reach. Rachmaninoff. Liszt."

He gave a little smile.

"Possibly. Possibly not. But we're talking about Bach."

"I guess I feel like it would be wrong to take it on if I don't have the capacity to play it as it's meant to be played. If you listen to Glenn Gould—"

Mr. Tate sat bolt upright. His hair bounced a few times, then settled.

"Glenn Gould, Miss Kippah, played almost nothing the way the composer meant it to be played. Glenn Gould was a genius of the highest caliber, and maybe the most important thing to happen to the Goldberg Variations in the twentieth century, but he's scared many a pianist away from them because of the way he played, crazy fast here, turtle slow there.

His renditions of Bach are utterly unique and will never be equaled. Nor should they be. But I am more interested in Moxie Roosevelt Kippah than Glenn Gould."

Wow. Miss Nimetz would have lay down and died on her living room rug before ever saying something like that.

"We're collaborating, you and I," Mr. Tate said. "So what we're going to work on together has to be agreeable to both of us. But here's what I'd like, Miss Kippah. I'd like to see you tackle Variation 28. And to do that, you have to leave the comfort of those ten pieces you play perfectly and be willing to get messy. Be comfortable with the sound of your own struggle as you try to work it out, even if it sounds like you're practicing with mittens on. Let it be a work in progress. The only way you're going to learn how to play it is to learn how *not* to play it first. The rest, Miss Kippah, is a simple process of elimination."

He folded his hands again and sat back, looking at me under slightly raised, huge white eyebrows.

The piece we were discussing was one I'd been avoiding for two years. I had never seen any reason to try and master something that seemed so clearly out of my reach.

But suddenly I felt a little loose, a little crazy.

"I can't believe I'm saying this, but yes. Yes, Mr. Tate. I'd like to give it a shot."

Mr. Tate beamed.

"I am not one bit surprised," he said. "We have our first regular lesson scheduled in"—he checked an appointment book on his desk—"in two days. Don't think about it until then. And for heaven's sake, put a nice cold can of Coca-Cola on that Gould recording, or use it as a bookmark, but don't listen to it."

I laughed. "I promise. No Gould."

"Mahvelous," he declared. "And now, I'm afraid I must run off. I've been charged with a very important duty, Miss Kippah, and that is to bring a potato salad to the Arts and Humanity faculty meeting this afternoon. Do you know the secret to an acceptable potato salad?"

I was not afraid to admit that I did not. I shook my head. Mr. Tate leaned forward with the air of someone about to impart extremely confidential and important information.

"A big blob of good mayonnaise," he said.

I laughed again.

"You Yankees have no sense of what constitutes good mayonnaise," he declared. "Fortunately, I make my own. I will see you in two days, Miss Kippah. I'm looking forward to working together."

"Likewise," I said.

I could have stayed in Mr. Tate's office all morning. I could have listened to his thoughts on everything from harpsichords to what was lacking in Yankee mayonnaise. But that would have to wait. I stood up at the same time he did.

"Have a pleasant aftahnoon, Miss Kippah," he drawled, leading me to the door.

Then he checked his watch.

"Pahdon me. Have a pleasant mawnin'."

I skipped like a third grader all the way back to my dorm, and I didn't even care who saw.

PERSONALITY LOGBOOK—
FOR REFERENCE ONLY

SATURDAY:
Personality: Detached, Unique, Coolly Knowing Individual (DUCKI). Alluded to possible criminal background in conversation with Spinky. Also mentioned plans to get a tattoo.

Personality: Mysterious Earth Goddess (MEG). Did not dispute Haven's belief that I am a Wicca practitioner (note to self: very brief Googling indicates that as a Wiccan, I worship the Great Goddess and the Horned God, and am a very good witch—better even than Glinda in "The Wizard of Oz"). FURTHER RESEARCH REQUIRED.

SUNDAY:
Personality: Hale and Hearty Sports Enthusiast (HHSE). Made tentative plans to watch the Yankees game with black-haired freshman with braces and long earlobes and first name sounding like Guadalupe. Agreed that the

team never fully recovered from the loss of someone named Herman Munster or Thurman Munson, and avowed core hatred of people who wear red socks.

MONDAY:

Personality: Assertive Revolutionary Activist (ARA). Mentioned to fellow freshman Sage Juliusburger that I spent the summer as a volunteer crew member on an oceanic sloop to publicize the environmental plight of the sea cow.

Personality: DUCK! Told sophomore Beverly Haagendoorf that I had been to Denmark several times and was locally considered to be somewhat of an expert on the differing aromas of Scandinavian cheeses.

chapter seven

Though Monday had technically been the first day of classes, they mostly consisted of our introducing ourselves and going over the syllabus. I was taking English lit, bio, French, American history, and algebra. I wasn't overly worried about most of it, except for the math.

My attempt over the weekend to review basic mathematical processes had culminated in using my algebra textbook as a practice keyboard. Worse, my algebra teacher, Mrs. Feeny, had the smallest mouth I'd ever seen, and she talked a mile a minute in a soft, high voice. It was frankly a bit worrying to watch the other students nodding each time she asked if she was being clear. I had not retained a single thing she said after "My name is Mrs. Feeny."

Today's class had not gone much better. Mrs. Feeny started right in on algebra, explaining how we found x or y while everybody around me nodded and took notes. Did they really understand what she was talking about? Were they all geniuses? By the end of the forty-minute period, I didn't think I could find an x or a y if they were painted in DayGlo pink on the broad side of a barn.

With math safely out of the way for another day, I walked across the quad to Dempsey Hall for my first and last Self-Confidence Through Comedy session, patting my pocket to make sure I had my Personality Log with me. I had been faithfully updating the log, and reviewed my notes for longer than I'd studied for my upcoming American history quiz.

I saw a familiar face coming toward me as I walked. It was Kate Southington, looking a little too thin in a "Live off the Grid" T-shirt. Something about her whole look seemed mismatched. Her jeans were ripped and looked genuinely grubby, but her boots looked expensive. She had a polyester NYPD ball cap on, but a pair of gold dangly earrings that looked real. We both slowed down as we approached each other, like two alpha male lions at a watering hole. I felt suddenly uncomfortable, for reasons I couldn't pinpoint.

"Hey Kate," I said, immediately deciding that her detachment called for some DUCKIness on my part. "How's it going?"

"Is Spinky in her room?" she asked.

Good to hear it, Kate. Yes, thanks for asking, I'm fine as well.

"Um, no, she wasn't a minute ago. Why?" I asked.

"I was thinking about heading into town to check out Vintage Tunage. I thought she might want to go."

I, apparently, did not factor into this equation.

"Oh," I said. "We actually went into town and checked out Vintage Tunage yesterday."

Spinky had suggested we visit the used CD store, and even advised me on my first purchase as a non-ordinary person—a retrospective collection by someone named Iggy Pop. Which sounded to me like it involved slippery balloons.

"*You* went to Vintage Tunage with Spinky?" Kate asked. It sounded like an accusation.

"Well, yeah," I said. I was trying to keep an even tone, but Kate was alarming me. "We signed out and got a bus pass and everything. Was there . . . I mean . . . um . . ."

"*We* were supposed to go," Kate said. "Spinky and I." She scowled at me. It was not a good look for her. Not a good look for me either.

"Oh," I said. "She didn't say anything. I mean, maybe she forgot. I mean, sorry."

Kate's scowl deepened.

"But we'll definitely be going back," I said quickly. "We could let you know when we—"

"Forget it," Kate said abruptly. "I'll talk to her myself."

She walked off quickly, leaving me standing there with a bad feeling in my stomach. Though I hadn't warmed at all to Kate, something told me she was not a person whose bad side you wanted to get on. And I had apparently just gotten on hers, by going to a CD store with my roommate.

Weird.

Well, it was not Detached or Unique or Coolly Knowing to stand there frozen like a sculpture, so I continued on toward Dempsey Hall, trying to put a spring in my step. When I had almost reached the door, I heard someone call my name. I looked around and saw a girl waving at me from the other side of the quad.

Black hair . . . black hair . . . calling something about a score . . .

"YanKEES!" I yelled, giving her the thumbs-up.

Guadalupe, if that was her name, returned my thumbs-up and mimed whipping an imaginary baseball at me.

"What about that thing at third base last night?" she called.

Having not actually watched or read about the game, I went for an oblique hand gesture that might have meant "nuts" or "hit in the head with a ball" or "I can't hear you," then dashed inside.

I didn't even have to check the Personality Log, I thought, pleased. I was on top of my facts, if nothing else. But I wasn't so sure about the Hale and Hearty Sports Enthusiast in general. I still loved the idea of having a team, especially since there were so many matching collectibles—T-shirts, mugs, Beanie Babies in ball caps, all with team logo. The only problem was I didn't like watching baseball all that much. Maybe I should try out for field hockey instead. Or soccer. The uniforms were awfully cute. But that meant after-school games and meets, which would cut into my practice time. My first lesson with Mr. Tate had been intense and occasionally hilarious, and left me more determined than ever to struggle through Variation 28. That meant plenty of time at the keyboard.

It was very quiet inside Dempsey Hall. The marble floors gleamed in the soft yellow light, as if they had been polished that very morning. I climbed a wide wooden staircase to the second floor and walked down the hallway, scanning the doors for the number 212. It was the last room on the left. The door was standing open, so I walked right in.

There was no one there. The room had high ceilings, white walls, and a large blackboard built into the front wall, on which someone had drawn a picture of two large cats walking upright. Desks were positioned in a circle around the room. I walked over to one of the tall windows that overlooked the inner campus. I hated that I was the first one there.

I stared out the window, mentally rehearsing what I would say to the teacher. I decided that as soon as she came in I'd go over to her so that we could speak privately. I didn't want to offend the other people in the EE, after all. Presumably they had all chosen Self-Confidence Through Comedy because they thought it sounded great. It was a nightmare only to me.

Where *were* the other kids, anyway? I looked at my watch. EE was supposed to start at 3:30, and according to my Timex it was 3:29. I pulled a folded piece of paper out of my pocket, where I'd written down the information for my EE. Dempsey 212. I was in the right room. Unless they'd made a typo on the sheet . . . Was I in the wrong place? How could everyone else have known to find the right room?

I was on the verge of panic when another girl walked into the room. A tiny girl. If I hadn't known EE was only for freshmen, I'd have guessed she was still in middle school based solely on her height. So when she spoke, she gave me a shock.

"Moxie Kipper? I'm Ms. Hay."

Ms. Hay? This elfin creature was a teacher? And how did she know I was Moxie?

"Hey," I said, then winced. It sounded like I was making fun of her name.

She smiled. She had a very wide mouth, or maybe it was normal sized but just looked wide because her head was so small. She had light brown hair in a pageboy, and small brown eyes. Her nose was slightly flat, and one nostril was bigger than the other. She was wearing a shirt woven with some kind of glittery thread, and black bell bottom jeans. Everything about her looked like a mistake. I tried not to stare.

"Welcome to Release Your Inner Stand-Up: Self-Confidence Through Comedy," Ms. Hay said, standing in the center of the classroom.

"Yes, right," I said. "I was hoping to talk to you about that before everyone else gets here."

"Actually, I think you *are* everybody," she said, glancing

at her clipboard. She held it up to show me. "Yep. You're it, Moxie Kipper."

I stared at the clipboard. The wind suddenly left my sails. Because there, as plain as day, was my signature. All theories of clerical errors evaporated.

Good grief. I had signed the wrong clipboard.

Ms. Hay watched me patiently. Here I was, her only taker. It was one thing to complain that the school had made a mistake. But the mistake was mine. I was the only person in the whole school who had signed up for her EE. How could I now tell her that I didn't want to take the class after all? There was no way for me to know if she'd even let me switch, or if Green You had any room left. The last thing I needed was to make a teacher mad at me this early in the school year.

"Moxie? Did you say you wanted to talk to me about something?"

Tell her, demanded an inner voice. *No! You CAN'T tell her*, yelled a second inner voice. *Say something!* cried both voices.

"Um . . . well . . ." I murmured, buying myself a little time.

Ms. Hay gave me an encouraging smile, which, I'm embarrassed to say, only made her look stranger than she already did. I suddenly felt terrible for Ms. Hay. She couldn't be more than four foot ten. Her eyes were too small and her nose looked squashed down and her clothes were . . . not so good either. Nobody was interested in her class but me, and even I wasn't interested.

"Well, it's just that actually, Ms. Hay . . . I'm not very funny."

Ms. Hay grinned at me. She looked like one of those hobbits from *The Lord of the Rings*.

"Well now, Moxie Kipper, you just take a seat and let me worry about that."

What could I do? I wasn't the kind of person to just walk out and leave her alone with no one enrolled.

So I sat down.

Ms. Hay closed the classroom door and went to the desk by the blackboard. Instead of sitting down behind it, though, she got up on top of it and sat with her legs pulled up under her, ankles crossed and knees pointing out.

"First of all, Moxie, given the—shall we say—exclusive size of the class, maybe you'd like to consider choosing a different seat."

I was basically sitting as far from Ms. Hay as it was physically possible to get without rearranging the furniture. I got up sheepishly and transferred to the desk closest to her.

My inner voice #1 informed me that this was all my

fault, because I had to go and be all *nice* and refuse to hurt the Hobbit's feelings. Inner voice #2 told inner voice #1 to shut up.

"Much better. Okay Moxie Kipper, let's get started. First off, tell me why you signed up for Self-Confidence Through Comedy."

Because I experienced a clipboard malfunction. Because I didn't want to hurt a Hobbit's feelings.

"Um, that's hard to say," I stalled.

"That's okay," she replied.

I tried to look at her without seeming like I was staring. She was just so . . . little. Not like the little people in *The Wizard of Oz*, not munchkin-esque . . . just on the tiniest possible edge of normal I'd ever seen.

"You're here, Moxie, and that's what's important. I could start by giving you a long-winded history of comedy, or I could go into a highbrow analysis of why being funny can be a powerful coping mechanism, or I could really milk the standard aphorisms like 'Laughter is the best medicine.' But I'm not going to."

Okay. Good.

Were we done, then?

"The essential fact is that whether you're a homecoming queen, a bookworm, a budding rocket scientist, or a teacher who's not much bigger than an American Girl doll, it always helps to be able to crack a joke every now and then."

Wait. That thing about the doll. Was she talking about *herself*?

Was I supposed to laugh?

"Some people think you're either born funny, or you're not. That isn't true. To be funny, you have to make a conscious choice to take a risk. Like singing, for example. You're potentially putting yourself out there to be judged, and if you care too much about that, it'll affect the sound of your voice. Self-Confidence Through Comedy is going to show you how to stop caring about how people react to your jokes. Once you do that, you stop caring about what people think of you altogether. So it's not so much teaching you how to be funny, which is impossible, as it is teaching you how not to care if sometimes you *aren't*."

What?

Ms. Hay gave me one of her huge, mildly alarming smiles.

"Don't worry. We'll figure it all out along the way. Let me just give you the information that we're all supposed to give students up front. Our EE is scheduled to meet every Tuesday and Thursday at three thirty in this classroom. I teach Latin and Greek history in this classroom, so if you ever need to find me and I'm not in my office, check here. Attendance for EE is mandatory unless you have a note from the Health Center. That's what it says on my memo. Between you and me, since it's just the two of us, we can always reschedule if something comes up, like you have a big paper due the next day, or you have a fight with your roommate, whatever. We just need to meet twelve times in the next six weeks.

"The second thing I'm supposed to tell you is about what they call the"—she referred to the paper she was holding—"Educational Enrichment Program Academic Community Participation Fulfillment. I don't know who makes up these names. Anyway, what it means is each EE has some public thing they have to do at Eaton in connection with what they're studying. Green You, for example, has to make a presentation at Morning Meeting on how to lessen your home environmental impact."

Why was Green You *constantly* reappearing in my life like an embarrassing uncle with a cologne-abuse problem?

"So your participation thing for this EE is pretty basic—all enrolled new students, that is *you*, have to do a five- to ten-minute presentation explaining what you've learned through this EE about how using humor can help us be more comfortable with who we are. It's a school-wide event at the New Student Talent Show, which is on Open Visit weekend for parents in October. That's all."

That's all? That's ALL?

I shook my head.

"No, I . . . see, no. I can't get up and perform in front of the school," I said.

"Why not?" Ms. Hay asked.

"Well, the thing is . . . you see. I . . . I'm . . . Amish."

Ms. Hay's eyes widened. Her gaze fell momentarily to my T-shirt, which was black with red letters reading: "Death Metal University." What can I say—I'd put it on this morning while sharing a DUCKI moment with Spinky.

"Amish?" she asked.

"Yes. It's a kind of religious community that you live in, very old-fashioned. We keep our homes and persons very plain—no electricity even."

"I know who the Amish are," Ms. Hay said, glancing at my T-shirt again. The corners of her mouth tugged up slightly.

"I see you've noticed the Death Metal University shirt," I said. "I wouldn't normally be wearing it. My roommate lent it to me."

That part was true.

"But while I'm at Eaton," I continued, "I'm . . . well, we Amish folks . . . this is a . . . um . . ."

"Your rumspringa?" Ms. Hay asked.

What? Was this a trap? Was rump springer a real word? Wait. Don't panic. Go with it.

"Well, that's what you English may call it," I said, trailing off.

"Hmmmm."

Keep talking, I told myself. But it was difficult. My stomach was doing a weird sort of flutter, like it was preparing to escape from the rest of my body.

"Right, so anyway, the Amish are okay with humor, sort of, I mean, smiling is definitely okay. But getting up onstage to make jokes and talk about myself is probably . . . Being humble is really important to us, and you know, being that my parents will probably be visiting that weekend, it could really shock them, and I'd hate for them to take the horse and buggy all this way only to feel . . . shamed."

Ms. Hay made an odd coughing sound while keeping her lips pressed firmly together. Then she cleared her throat.

"Well, it is a requirement of the class," she said. "And there are many ways to be funny without being offensive. I'm here to teach you humor as a coping mechanism, to be comfortable with who you are. Speaking publicly is part of that. Take me, for example. If I have to make an announcement in Morning Meeting, I have to bring a little box to stand on so I can reach the microphone. Now, I could try to do that discreetly, or I could make a joke out of it. Being extremely short is part of who I am. I own it by seeing the humor in it."

Wow. That was sort of impressive, although I had no idea what personality that made her. She was clearly not a DUCKI or a MEG or any of the other classifications on my list. What was she? Or did standard personalities not apply to teachers?

"So I feel certain that you can learn something in this class, Moxie. Even with your . . . Amish limitations."

Oh.

"Okay," I mumbled. I was trapped. What else could I do?

"Okay, then. I think that's probably it for today. The students always say the shorter, the better," Ms. Hay said. "I think that's why I'm so popular. So I'll see you on Thursday, Moxie."

She just sat there on top of the desk, like a collectible Buddha paperweight. But she'd said we were done, so I got up.

"Bye," I said. Then I walked as Amishly as possible out the door and into the hallway.

I felt like I had pulled that off okay. But it had all been for nothing, because I was still going to have to get up in front of the entire school and perform. How nauseating and potentially stupid. Everyone would . . .

I froze in my tracks. Performing in front of *the entire school*. Together in one room at the same time. Some of them thought I was a DUCKI, some believed I was a MEG, several figured I was an ARA or a HHSE, and I'd just told one I was Amish.

Well then.

I had a problem.

Chapter Eight

By nearly the end of the first week and with two sessions under my belt, I still wasn't sure I could live with Self-Confidence Through Comedy. Ms. Hay seemed nice enough, but I couldn't stop silently agonizing about my unwilling upcoming comedy debut. I was mulling it over again in the lunch line when someone tapped me on the shoulder. I turned around to see a smiling girl with brown hair and bright blue eyes. Sage Juliusburger. I could always remember her name right away because we both lived in Sage.

"Hey, Moxie," she said, smiling. She turned to the person behind her. "I want you to meet my roommate. Reagan, this is the girl I was telling you about—the one who crewed on the sloop this summer to publicize the plight of the sea cow."

Reagan shot into view next to Sage. It was a good thing I'd just gone over the Personality Log. The sloop scenario was nothing if not detail-heavy, and the name "sea cow" had popped into my head so randomly I could never come up with it again without notes.

"Hey, I've been dying to meet you!" she exclaimed.

She was of medium height and build, with shoulder-length brown hair and large intelligent eyes behind thick glasses. I didn't get an immediate read on her. Her glasses said brain. Her Bean boots said preppie. Her black T-shirt said possibly prone to brooding. The wide silver cuff bracelet on her wrist said expensive. On her dinner tray she was carrying a small glass bowl containing two little fish. That said . . . eccentric. I couldn't stop myself from staring at the bowl as the fish swam in lazy little circles.

"I didn't want to leave them alone in my room," Reagan explained when she saw me looking at the fish. "I decided to take them for a walk so they could experience other life forms. They've had a very difficult day."

"What constitutes a difficult day for your fish?" I asked.

"They're not *my* fish," Reagan stated.

"Oh. Okay. I thought you said . . ."

"The fish and I are together. But they are not *my* fish."

I didn't say anything, which is often an excellent tactic

when you have no idea what someone is talking about.

"Reagan doesn't believe that humans should assert ownership over animals," Sage explained. "She won't even eat meat."

"Oh, of course. No. Me neither. Right! But where'd you get them?" I asked. "I mean, how did they come into your company?"

"I liberated them from a flea market in town yesterday," Reagan said. "I spent my last five dollars trying to toss three Ping-Pong balls into one of their bowls to 'win them,' as the vendor put it. As far as I'm concerned, they won me. So these fish and I are temporarily hanging together until I can reintroduce them into the wild."

"That's great!" I exclaimed.

This was kind of along the lines of my old plan to liberate lobsters from fish sellers. As far as I was concerned, Reagan was good people.

"So I want to hear about your experience on the sloop!" Reagan said eagerly. "What did you do?"

We had reached the selection of entrees. I bought some time by examining the meatloaf with a serious eye.

"Well, I was an apprentice. Apprentice to the . . . swabber."

"I know beans about sailing, sorry," Reagan said. "What's a swabber do?"

I shook my head, like it was all too technical to get into.

"Just basic, you know. Swabbing. Everything needs swabbing in the salt air, right?"

"I could never swab," Sage said, a little ruefully. "I'd get seasick."

"Me neither. But the sea cow . . . I've never heard of them. Are they an endangered species?" Reagan asked. She knitted her eyebrows in a worried way.

Without giving it any real thought, I took a piece of meatloaf and dropped it onto my plate. It made kind of a smacking sound, followed by a resounding silence. I looked up to see Reagan watching me with a confused frown. Had I splattered her with gravy? Taken too large a slice? Was there something wrong with the meatlo . . . Meatloaf. Meat. I was a vegetarian sea cow activist, committing the ultimate sin. *Think fast, think fast!*

"The tofu-loaf looks a little weird, doesn't it?" I asked. It was a shame I wasn't wearing my "I Love Tofu" T-shirt to lend some helpful weight to my words.

A look of relief crossed Reagan's face. "Oh, Moxie, that isn't tofu-loaf. It's actually meat," she said.

I stared at the plate in horror.

"What?" I asked, trying to look indignantly shocked. I grabbed the plate and put it back on the counter, shoving it as far away from me as I could.

"Try the eggplant Parmesan, maybe," Sage suggested.

"Great idea," I said, helping myself.

The taste of eggplant made me a little sick, but maybe I could just eat the cheese off the top and no one would be the wiser.

With the entrée disaster now averted, I followed my two new friends to a table.

"So I hear you have a missing roommate," Sage said.

"Yeah, I guess she's coming later in the semester," I said.

"I hear she released some kind of virus from a Petri dish in the bio lab and they had to burn all the desks," Sage said.

I hesitated.

"I'm not exactly sure what happened with her," I said carefully. A virus?

"So you were talking about the sea cow? Being endangered?" Reagan prompted as we sat down.

"What? Well, yeah!" I said. "Because the sea cow subsists, of course, by, um . . . grazing."

"Grazing?" asked Sage. In spite of her suggestion, she had avoided the eggplant and grabbed a mixed salad. I eyed it jealously.

"Yes. So the recent decline in the uh . . . the algae pastures . . . affects the ability to graze efficiently. You know how it goes."

"There's nothing for them to eat?" Sage asked, pausing with her fork halfway to her mouth. She looked ready to pack up her salad and ship it off to the sea cows immediately.

I shook my head. Reagan looked like she might cry.

"That's terrible! There are so many species of animals that are suffering like this, mostly because of humans. We've spent the last century or two creating obstacle after obstacle to the ecosystem with our self-interested industry and technology. Why can't more people understand that we owe animals our help?" Reagan asked. She paused with emotion, her lower lip quivering a little.

I was starting to feel mighty bad for these sea cows myself, forgetting momentarily that I had invented them along with their imaginary algae pastures. And then I felt even worse. There were plenty of real animals on the endangered list, after all. Now I had invented a new species and practically destroyed it in only a few minutes. Not an ideal start for a budding animal rights activist. The whole thing made my stomach hurt.

"Let's not talk about the sea cow," I said. "It's depressing. Besides . . ."

Then I gestured toward her fish. Like, it might *upset* them. The smaller one did look a little agitated around the eyes.

"But that's exactly why we *do* have to talk about it," Reagan insisted. "We need to face the painful stuff the last generation has left for us, or we'll never be able to deal with it ourselves!"

Uh-oh. My subject-change cue had failed.

"And I'm sorry to say I'm as ignorant as anyone about this sea cow situation," Reagan continued. "I mean, where is their primary habitat? How many of them are there? Do you know what percentage of the population has died off?"

I was now officially in over my head. And the sea cows were circling. My ARA personality was in jeopardy—I recognized that. But there was too much going on in my mind at once. I opened my mouth, and then closed it with an audible click. What I really needed to do was get to the practice rooms as soon as possible. If I knew anything about my real self, it was that when things got crazy, the best thing I could do was pound things out on the ivories for an hour or two. Or at least for a half hour before French.

"The truth is, Reagan," I said, taking a deep breath and hoping the truth was about to hit me, "the truth is, in actuality, in the starkest possible terms . . ."

I leaned forward as if I was going to tell her a secret, and with my body blocking her view, I tipped my twelve-ounce glass of milk into my own lap.

"Oh, gosh! Darn!" I yelled, leaping up.

The good news was the subject of the sea cow population was momentarily tabled. The bad news was that just about everybody was now looking at me.

Reagan and Sage handed me all of their napkins.

"I'm so sorry, you guys," I said. "What a klutz. I better go to my room and get cleaned up."

"Sure!" Reagan said, tossing some extra napkins onto the floor to mop up the excess. "Maybe I'll find you later. One of the reasons I wanted to meet you is I'm planning on starting an animal rights group," she said. "I'm going to petition the administration to start my own. And to fund me. Not as an EE, since those end after October, but as a school club. Do you think you might be able to help me out?"

"Definitely!" I said, squirming in my soaking jeans. "I'm definitely in. I'll catch you later, okay?"

"Great!" Reagan exclaimed. "Maybe someone in your sea cow group could send us a letter of recommendation."

"Maybe," I told Reagan. "Or there's this environmental guy my mom did some writing for last year—Julius Severay, I think his name is."

Reagan's mouth dropped wide open.

"Julius Severay? Of the Global Wildlife Coalition?"

"That's the guy."

"My gosh, he's like, huge!"

"I can ask my mom to e-mail him. See if he'd be willing to get you a letter, or endorsement or something."

Reagan put her hand over her mouth.

"That would be . . . Oh Moxie . . . that would be the coolest thing ever!"

"I'll get right on it," I said with a grin.

Reagan patted her roommate's arm.

"You were right, Sage. This girl is aces."

Sage smiled.

I gave them both what I felt was an excellent Assertive Revolutionary Activist smile—strong, compassionate, and committed. Well, that's what I was aiming for, anyway. And I meant it. In spite of the mess I'd made over the sea cow thing, not to mention the milk, I realized that being an ARA was extremely inspiring. This was definitely a top contender for my new personality, if I could just get things under control again.

I walked toward the dining hall exit, my wet sneakers making a high squeaking sound. As I reached the doorway, my path was blocked by someone trying to come in at the same time. Kate Southington. There was a brief, weird moment where I expected us to engage in the little step-left-step-right dance you do when you're trying to get around someone. But Kate stood stock-still, like she was made of marble. I was torn between a Mexican stand-down and avoiding an awkward moment in public. After a few seconds, I opted for avoiding the awkward moment and got out of the way. Kate began to breeze past me like royalty, pausing to direct a quick, pointed stare at my milk-sodden jeans. I felt a flash of irritation at myself for giving in so easily.

So I guess this was the way it was going to be now. I had a hint of it the night before, when Kate showed up in our suite to invite Spinky over for cake. Just Spinky. Spinky, always congenial, had cheerfully accepted the offer, generously suggesting that I might like to come along. But one glance at the scowl on Kate's face was enough. I made a polite excuse about having to investigate some classic Iggy Pop cuts on iTunes. When they walked out, Kate put her arm through Spinky's and shot me a look I can only describe as triumphant. She seemed to think that Spinky was a prize we were competing for. And that only one of us could win. I refused to now simply stand frozen like a dummy.

So I loudly said hello to her. My mother always says the best way to deal with someone who's being hostile is to be nice to them. The best way to deal with Kate, then, was to be nice to her no matter what she did to me.

And it worked, because like most people, Kate had the

automatic-response-impulse hardwired into her brain, which caused her to look over her shoulder and say hello back to me when she probably would have preferred to maintain an icy silence. But she ducked her head after she said it, and turned her face in the other direction, reminding me of a celebrity encountering hordes of photographers.

"Well, see you later," I said, making my tone cheerful. "Watch out for those paparazzi!"

Now, I don't know why I said that last part. I guess I was still thinking Kate looked like a movie star ducking an *Entertainment Television* cameraman. I certainly didn't mean anything by it. But she turned around and glared at me with such hostility, I almost gasped. It was crazy! How could anyone be insulted by that ridiculous remark?

The be-nice-to-your-enemies thing was clearly off the table for now. I did what any normal person would do— I fled, trotting as fast as I could into the alcove, then heading for the hallways. Auntie Sparkles gave me a disapproving look as my shoes squeaked while I jogged up the stairs. I'm sure she felt running was un-ladylike, as was being covered with milk.

But the practice rooms were clear across campus— I had to put on some dry pants and get to a piano before I accidentally-on-purpose made a bigger mess of my life.

PERSONALITY LOGBOOK—
FOR REFERENCE ONLY

TUESDAY:

Late morning:

Personality: HHSE. Borrowed copy of "The Shaquille O'Neil Story" from library and placed it on top of book bag with title visible during all morning classes.

American history:

Personality: ARA. Muttered darkly under breath and squeezed both hands into fists when teacher made brief mention of the percentage of global warming directly attributable to choice of personal vehicle.

Sometime after 3:00:

Personality: Unknown. Told Ms. Hay I was Amish.

WEDNESDAY:

Lunch:

Personality: DUCKI. Visited school bookstore

and loitered in the poetry section, leafing through "Anarchy and Atheists: A Poetic Anthology for the Ages."

Before dinner:
Personality: MEG. Snacked on tofu crisps in student lounge and remarked loudly on their delicious, wholesome, and nutty flavor and their admirable lack of trans fats and "yellow #5 lake," or other bizarre food coloring occurring naturally only in Skittles.

THURSDAY:
Personality: ARA. Told Reagan the sea cow population has dwindled due to reduced algae pastures. Promised to be in her animal club! Also, investigate qualifications necessary to be promoted to Full Swabber.

Chapter Nine

I skipped dinner. I didn't want to run into Kate, it's true. Also, I have an embarrassing appetite for *Fabulous* magazine, the fat glossy monthly that delivered all the food groups: beauty tips, makeovers, horoscopes, and celebrity gossip. I wanted to get to the school bookstore before it closed to buy the latest issue. The Eaton bookstore was a miracle of commerce—they carried everything from T-shirts and sweats emblazoned with the school logo, to school supplies, unhealthy snacks, assorted toiletries, textbooks, actual books, and a generous selection of magazines.

I arrived at the bookstore with cash in pocket, ready to feed my *Fabulous* habit, only to find Luscious Luke standing in front of the magazine rack, absorbed in something about video gaming. Luscious Luke was almost as flawless as Carson McGillion. In addition to being the son of Eaton's Dean of Students, he was high profile for his glorious floppy blond hair, his thickly curled eyelashes, his long lanky legs, and for being the only teenage boy on campus. Luscious Luke didn't know me from a jelly donut, but I'd have sooner gone to the dentist for a couple of root canals than buy *Fabulous* in front of him.

I realized I'd have to stall until he left. So I made a beeline around the bookshelves in the opposite direction of the magazine rack and almost collided with a very small person in an oversized ball cap bearing a Chicago Bears logo.

"Yowza," said Ms. Hay.

"I'm so sorry," I said. "I didn't see you. I mean, I wasn't looking," I corrected quickly, because I didn't want to make it sound like a comment about her height.

"Happens to me all the time," Ms. Hay said. "That's life when your head doesn't even clear the top of the 'contemporary romance novel' stack."

She laughed, and I responded with an uncomfortable smile.

One of the weird things about boarding school is getting used to seeing your teachers outside of the classroom. It wasn't always a good thing. I had run into Mrs. Feeny outside the gym complex just the day before. I never enjoyed seeing Mrs. Feeny under any circumstances, and now that the vision of her in spandex running pants was burned into my retinas, I liked it even less.

But for some reason Ms. Hay didn't give me that same squirmy get-me-out-of-here feeling. And since Luscious Luke was now near the door, it was a bad time to make a quick getaway. I decided to buy a few seconds by remarking on the books Ms. Hay had tucked under one arm.

"Um, find something good?" I asked.

Ms. Hay heaved an enormous sigh.

"Busted," she said.

"Busted?" I asked. Who was busted?

She scanned the bookstore for eavesdroppers carefully with an exaggerated expression, then leaned toward me.

"Promise. Not. To. Tell," she whispered.

I nodded. It was easy, given I had no idea what we were talking about.

"Okay," Ms. Hay said. Then she showed me the books.

"*Star Trek* novels?" I exclaimed.

Ms. Hay hung her head.

"My secret shame," she said. Then she looked up at me and winked.

"You're a Trekkie," I said.

She nodded.

"Card-carrying," she added.

"My dad says being a Trekkie is a sign of intelligence," I said. He really had said that. More than once.

"Well obviously, he's right," she said. Then she lowered her voice to a theatrical whisper. "But not everyone . . . you know. Understands."

I laughed.

"Well . . . we . . . Amish are known for our . . . understanding and stuff," I said.

"I certainly appreciate it," Ms. Hay said very seriously.

"Well, it's not like you're one of those nutbags who wears a Starfleet uniform and speaks Klingon and stuff," I said.

Ms. Hay held her arms out like wings, a Star Trek novel clutched in each miniature hand.

"Hello. My name is Nutbag."

"You . . . have a Starfleet uniform?" I asked, trying not to laugh at the idea.

"Original series, the red one Uhura used to wear. I've even got the go-go boots and a communicator to go with it. I'm still working on the Klingon, though."

Ms. Hay looked like she was bursting with pride in the face of this disclosure. My mind was tumbling over and over again trying to get a visual image of Starfleet Cadet Hay. It was an oddly adorable picture.

"Well, I liked the newest movie," I offered.

Oh. Did the Amish go to movies?

Ms. Hay shot one hand up, palm out.

"Stop right there," she commanded. "I don't want to hear about that film. If you want real *Star Trek,* you've got to go back to the sixties."

Something about the gleam in her eyes made me want to do so immediately.

"Maybe I can rent it over vacation," I said.

"Forget renting it," Ms. Hay said. "I've got it all on DVD. Three seasons in three boxes shaped like photon torpedoes: command yellow, science blue, and engineering red. Tell you what—after what I'm sure will be your EE talent show triumph, I'll have you over to check out a few choice episodes. We can watch and nosh. I make a mean Beanie Weenie."

Oh my god. I *loved* Beanie Weenie.

"Definitely," I said.

Ms. Hay gave me a grin. Then her expression became more serious. "Parents still aren't going to be able to make it?" she asked.

"Oh. Well, I think not," I said. "It would be very difficult." Because I hadn't told them about the talent show. And hoped I could get away with *never* telling them.

"That's too bad," she said. "Well, Amish Moxie, I'll see you in EE, then. Don't forget to do your reading."

"Already done," I told her.

Amish Moxie sort of had a ring to it. How did a person get to be Amish, anyway? Was there a written exam?

"Excellent."

She shot me the hard-to-do finger sign the Vulcans make, and headed over to the cash register.

I was inspired. I would buy my *Fabulous* magazine even if Luscious Luke himself was working the register. Fortunately, a quick scan of my surroundings indicated he had finally left. The coast was clear.

But minutes later, after checking the magazine racks top to bottom, and even looking behind the news weeklies, I still had nothing.

Well, if Ms. Hay could take her *Star Trek* novels to the checkout lady, I could make a simple inquiry.

"Do you carry *Fabulous* magazine?" I asked in my DUCKIest voice.

The checkout lady tapped a few keys on her computer.

"New issue ships in a few days. Check back."

I thanked the woman, and sighed.

Fabulous magazine was my best hope at temporarily checking out of my the-talent-show-is-coming reality. I actually envied Ms. Hay her *Star Trek* mania at the moment. I needed something to distract me from my life on Planet Complicated. Ideally, I needed Starfleet's most colorful Chief Engineer Scotty to beam me out of the small mess I had gotten myself into. A girl could dream.

chapter Ten

When I got back to my room, Spinky was nowhere to be seen. Maybe she got permission to work in the library during study period. I deflated a little. I was so full of things to update her on—Ms. Hay's Starfleet uniform and my unwitting entrapment in the horrifying talent show, which we hadn't had a chance to talk about yet, the crazy and crazier Kate, the near-disastrous sea cow conversa . . .

Wait, what was I thinking? I couldn't tell Spinky about the sea cow debacle! I couldn't tell anyone. I sat down heavily at the empty desk. Suddenly I wanted nothing more than to tell Spinky everything.

I sighed and decided to focus on getting some work done. By the end of evening study period, I was surprised to find I'd been especially industrious, completing my

American history essay an impressive three days before it was due. When the bell rang, I dashed downstairs to the phone room to lob in a quick call to my mother (no cell phones allowed at Eaton). I was e-mailing her a few times a day, but I knew she appreciated a little voice-to-voice contact. And I didn't mind it so much either. When I got back upstairs, the door to my room was open, and I could hear laughter coming from inside.

Spinky had emerged from her own studying session, and was lounging on the still-unclaimed bed in the middle room, flanked by Haven and Reagan.

"There she is," Spinky declared, pointing one blue-nailed, silver-ringed finger at me. "Roomie, the whole world has stopped by to visit you."

I beamed. I didn't think Reagan and Haven constituted "the whole world" by any stretch of the imagination, but I was flattered and pleased beyond words that they'd both decided to stop by my room. Still, I didn't want to air the horror of my first week to everyone. It would just have to wait.

"Wow, hey!" I said, pulling up a chair and sitting opposite them like a talk show host. "I just had to call my mom. You know how it is," I added.

Reagan nodded. "I'm on the everyday plan myself," she said. "At least for the first week."

"We don't have phones at the ashram," Haven said. "Except for in the office."

"You live on an ashram?" Spinky exclaimed, staring at Haven with intense interest. Reagan leaned forward and examined Haven too.

"That is extremely cool," Reagan said.

"*Extremely* cool," I declared, wishing with deep despair that I knew what an ashram was.

"So is it—" Reagan started, while at the same time Spinky said, "What kind of—"

They laughed and broke off simultaneously, then for some reason both looked at me.

"Well, do tell," I said to Haven, in an exaggerated Southern accent—after two lessons with Mr. Tate, I couldn't help it. Also, there seems to be something about a Southern accent that, when used correctly, can disguise the fact that what you're saying really makes no sense. I'd used it in math classes all my life, and it worked like a charm here.

"There's not that much to tell, really," Haven said, pulling her long hair around one shoulder. "It's a Buddhist community, mostly following the Tibetan Gelugpa tradition. My parents helped found it back in the seventies. We have about thirty acres in northern Vermont. We grow most of our own food, and sell the rest to the local organic markets . . ." She looked around at us thoughtfully. "Most of the kids are homeschooled, but my grandparents have been pushing my parents to try me here by promising to foot the bill. We get Tibetan teachers to come sometimes and do meditation retreats, which are open to the public. It's quiet . . . We're pretty much off the grid."

"That. Is. Outstanding!" Reagan exclaimed.

There's something really neat that happens when you introduce people you like to other people you like and they all really like each other. I felt like I'd filled the house at Carnegie Hall.

"*I* want to live on an ashram," Spinky declared.

I enjoyed a quick vision of Spinky mingling with a bunch of Buddhists. They'd probably love each other.

"Well, you can come visit anytime," Haven said. "All of you can."

"Let's!" Reagan said. "We should all go together!"

"I cannot promise to eat tofu," Spinky warned.

"There's more than just tofu. Take my word for it," Haven said.

"I love tofu. So does Moxie," Reagan said.

"So her T-shirt claims," Spinky said. "I thought it was irony."

Uh-oh. I put a scandalized expression on my face.

"I live and breathe tofu," I said very loudly, so that it could be interpreted as a joke, or as the truth delivered

113

with mock seriousness. "And I have the T-shirt to prove it."
We needed to get off the subject of food and my "I Love
Tofu" shirt, though, because I had gone on at length about
my love of corn dogs to Spinky earlier that very day.

"You should join Reagan's animal rights group, Haven,"
I said. "You guys both should."

"I'm a total animal rights booster. Count me in," Spinky
said. She rubbed one hand over her green brush cut. "Can
I be on the little rubber boat that goes between the whales
and the harpooning ships?"

"You absolutely can," Reagan said. "I'm, well, still in the
planning stages here. I have to get the school to okay the
club and give it some funding, for starters. But one day I
will totally sponsor a whale hunting intervention, and you
can be on it."

"Captain Spinky," Spinky said, smiling with satisfaction.
"Haven, is it true you can be reincarnated as an animal if
you're bad in this lifetime?"

This got Reagan's attention instantly, and mine too.
Haven gave us a slow smile.

"There's a monastery in Tibet where all these stray dogs
go to be fed," Haven said. "And the monks there believe
all those dogs are the reincarnations of monks who were
disgraced sometime in a former life. They take care of every
dog that comes to them, even if they have to go with less

food themselves, because they believe each animal was once like them. And that they could one day become like those animals."

There was a moment of silence as the three of us contemplated this rather remarkable image.

"So being a dog is like a demotion?" I asked.

Haven shook her head. "Not necessarily. There's a monk who comes to our ashram who believes that when he has achieved all the merit he needs to eradicate his bad karma as a human, he will come back for one final life as a yew tree—and that will be his reward for every other lifetime he's ever lived."

Reagan closed her eyes.

"That's the most beautiful thing I have ever heard," she said, a bit fiercely.

"It is," Spinky agreed quietly.

"I'd be a cedar tree," I said.

There was such a long silence that I started to panic, thinking I'd either said something unintentionally insulting, or my MEG hadn't matched up with my DUCKI and my ARA, and everyone was now staring at me cross-eyed.

"I'd be a redwood," Spinky chimed in after a while.

"I think I'd like to be a banyan tree," Haven said thoughtfully.

"Does it have to be a tree?" Reagan asked.

Haven shook her head, smiling with her eyes distant.

"Then I want to be a dolphin," Reagan said softly. "The kind that saves drowning people even though human beings are killing us with their fishing nets and their trash-dumping and their noise pollution. Even if I'm the last one left. I'll still try to help. And maybe one day the humans would learn something from me."

There was a long silence.

"So here we are—three future trees and a dolphin," I declared.

For the second time in several minutes, as soon as I spoke I thought I'd made a major blunder, somehow saying something so inappropriate and offensive that no one would ever forgive me. Was I crazy to think I could keep it together with my varying personalities when these three very different girls were in the same place at the same time?

But then Spinky and Reagan started to laugh, and Haven joined in with her bell-like little giggle.

"Captain Spinky is happy," Spinky said, leaning back. "Captain Spinky is going to save as many whales as she can."

Reagan sighed.

"More power to you. They are such magnificent creatures, so intelligent. One day I think we'll look back at our history and be absolutely appalled that we ever took part in slaughtering them."

Reagan's laughter had faded, and I noticed her eyes filling with tears. I felt something tug in my heart to think of this intense girl feeling so deeply. I decided to temporarily abandon my ban on classical music references, because I knew she'd love what I was thinking.

"There's this composer named Alan Hovanhess," I said suddenly, "and he wrote a symphonic piece called 'And God Created the Great Whale.' I heard it performed at Avery Fisher Hall once when I was little, and I swear, it was like I could actually feel the whales' energy in the music. It's like he found this unique combination of instruments and rhythm and tone that *were* the whales."

"Seriously? I have to hear it! Is it on iTunes?" Reagan asked eagerly.

"I have the CD. I'll lend it to you."

I went into my room and found the CD right away, because I'm very strict about keeping my music alphabetically by composer. When I went back to the middle room and handed it to Reagan, she took it carefully and stared at it like it was a winning lottery ticket.

"Moxie, thank you so much," Reagan said.

I actually blushed a little. "You're totally welcome," I said.

"Y'all are some seriously good people," Spinky announced.

And that included me. I, Moxie Roosevelt, and my new

friends, were some seriously good people. Spinky Spanger said so.

"Hey guys, you know what?" I asked. "Let's—"

There was a knock on the open door and I looked up to see Kate Southington standing in the doorway. I felt a wave of dismay. Kate looked as unhappy to see our bonding session as I was to see her. She stood, seeming uncertain what to do, a slight scowl on her face.

"Hey Kate, come on in," Spinky called cheerfully.

Or don't, I thought.

"Hey Spinky," Kate said. Apparently nobody else in the room rated a mention.

I felt sulky, then guilty, then finally summoned the will to be nice.

"I can get a chair from the other room," I offered.

"No thanks," Kate said.

She preferred to stand in the middle of the room, like an art installation that demanded attention.

There was a brief silence. *Nice*, I reminded myself.

"So what kind of tree are *you*, Kate?" I asked, shooting Haven a quick smile.

Kate looked at me, lips scrunched. "What?"

"What kind of tree are you? I mean, will you be? What kind of tree would you pick? Actually, it doesn't have to be a tree. You can be anything you want. Your choice. You're a blank slate."

Kate's scowl deepened into full hostility, and I shifted uncomfortably in my chair.

"See, we were all just talking about . . . Haven said that . . . Well. Never mind. I guess you had to be there." I gave up.

Ugh, she was awful! Like a Béla Bartók concerto—unpredictable and to my ear downright unpleasant. My attempt at niceness was officially over.

"Spink, I just came to see if you wanted to show me the old tunnels, the ones you and I were talking about? You were going to show me where they are."

Spinky half sat up.

"Oh, yeah. You mean now?"

"Yes," Kate said firmly.

There was a pause. Obviously no one else was going to be issued an invitation. I certainly didn't want to go anywhere with Kate Southington anyway.

"I should probably start getting my notes together for my presentation to the dean," Reagan said. "I have to do the pitch for the club in a few weeks, and I need it to be a slam dunk."

"Okay then," Spinky said, standing up. "The tunnels it is."

Reagan and Haven stood up too, so I followed suit.

"Catch you all later then," I said in a cheerful voice.

Haven flashed me a peace sign and glided out of the room. Reagan took a step toward the door, then turned and walked over to me, surprising me with a brief but intense hug.

"I'm really glad I met you, Mox," she said. "You're exactly the kind of person I was hoping to find for my club. And to be friends with. I thought Eaton would be full of fakers, but you are the real deal."

I couldn't do anything but smile. And I kept smiling as Reagan followed Spinky and Kate out the door, rendered frozen by the feeling of guilt that overcame me, and the knot that arrived in my stomach.

I was not exactly the real deal. But I comforted myself by thinking that I was not exactly *not* the real deal either. The thing is, I *intended* to become the person Reagan thought I already was.

And I knew a perfect way to start.

To: GreenDallas@newearth.net

From: Keyboardwiz@newearth.net

Hi Mom:

Thanks for forwarding the video and let's definitely see the movie when I'm on vacay—yes, I hate the way he looks without his beard too. Only have a sec right now—quick question/favor: There is this amazing girl here named Reagan Andersen you will love. She's putting together a proposal to get funding for a school animal rights club—I am going to help her out. Any chance you could get Julius Severay to e-mail a little something saying she's cool, or some such? Her e-mail is AllCreatures@arr.net. I totally vouch for her character . . . If he says yes, I will totally rub your feet every night of winter break.

Love, Mox

Chapter Eleven

Midway through my second week at Eaton, I was finally starting to get into the flow. I had classes every day, two early-morning lessons a week with Mr. Tate, and then EE. This left most of my afternoons free to work in the practice rooms. I'd started using the same one each time, and there were little cubbies there where I could store my music and my metronome, so I didn't have to schlep them around campus and out myself as an Über Piano Nerd.

I got up really early on Friday morning while Spinky was still fast asleep and headed over to the practice rooms to exercise my fingers and mull some things over in my brain before my 8:00 lesson with Mr. Tate. I warmed up with a series of Bach two-part Inventions, then took a deep breath and plunged into the first page of Goldberg

Variation number 28. It was physically painful to listen to the sound of my own playing. When I made it to the measure where Mr. Tate had told me to stop, I went back to the beginning and blundered through it again, wincing at the racket. By the time I arrived at Mr. Tate's office, I had gotten slightly used to sounding like I was playing with most of my fingers taped together.

"Ah, good mawnin' Miss Kippah," Mr. Tate said, standing up and giving me a little bow. "Ah, but—" He checked his watch, and beamed. "Good mawnin'," he repeated. One of the many things I'd learned from Mr. Tate in the last two weeks was that he often didn't sleep at night, but spent the hours listening to his old records, playing his piano, or working on compositions of his own. His perpetual confusion about the time was, I had decided, 60 percent real and 40 percent a put-on. He often professed the same confusion about the month, and occasionally the year. I loved 100 percent of it.

"How's our iceberg?" he asked. He'd taken to referring to the piece as our iceberg, though I was never quite clear if I was supposed to be the *Titanic,* the captain, or Kate Winslet. I like to think it was option number three.

"Cold, slippery, unpredictable, and full of cracks," I told him.

Mr. Tate clapped. "Perfect," he said. "Let's hear it."

"Okay, but—"

He raised one hand palm out, traffic-cop style, and I smiled. We had agreed on a strict "no disclaimers" policy for my playing—I was not supposed to apologize in avance for mistakes, blunders, or even flat-out disasters. I closed my mouth, sat down at the piano, took a deep breath, and played what I had been practicing for two days. When I finished, I sighed and looked over at him.

"Miss Kippah," Mr. Tate said, "I am extremely pleased that you have chosen to take my advice and leave the issue of finger precision for a later time."

I laughed. Only Mr. Tate could turn "Well, you hit plenty of wrong notes" into a compliment.

"And your trills are coming along. You may not hear it yet, but you are beginning to understand this variation. The tempo is good for you, it will come up to speed on its own, and you will be surprised at how fast you will move without giving the air of being showy."

"Liberace lived for showy," I said with a grin. Mr. Tate had a deep-seated loathing for the now-departed Las Vegas pianist, with his massive ringed fingers and sequin-covered coats.

"Liberace was about as sharp as a sack of wet mice," Mr. Tate declared. "All right, then, Miss Kippah. You've come a long way in just a few days, and I can tell without asking that you've been practicing up a storm. Now let's get down to business. Break the notes down, starting with this measure here."

I lost myself in the notes, seeing them through Mr. Tate's eyes, and before I knew it, the lesson was over. The lessons were never long enough, but they charged me like solar panels absorbing the sun and kept me going for the whole day.

I retained my good mood, even through an algebra class that I was certain Mrs. Feeny was conducting in Norwegian. In fact, the only two things at Eaton I was really unhappy with were math and Kate Southington. The sting of her obvious dislike of me gnawed away at all of my personalities, since I didn't believe I had done anything to deserve it. Part of me still wanted to try to win her over, because the whole situation made me uncomfortable.

And there was also the lingering specter of the New Student Talent Show, which I was beginning to think of as a horror movie called *The Thing That Was Not Funny*, starring me.

I could feel the pressure building, but I'd already spent all morning in the practice rooms. I needed something else. Oh, *Fabulous*! I made another stealth run to the school bookstore, which was full of students, most of whom were wearing soccer uniforms. One of them wasn't, however. I recognized Kate's strawberry blond ponytail and bony shoulders from the back. Should I pretend I didn't see her, or once again dip my toe in the icy waters of diplomacy?

The question answered itself when she turned around with a stack of magazines in her hands.

The magazine on top was *Fabulous*.

Finally—something to bond over!

"Why, Kate Southington, I'm onto you," I said cheerfully. "You can't hide from me."

Kate's head snapped around, and when she caught sight of me she looked positively alarmed.

I walked right over to her.

"Don't worry," I said, nodding my head toward the magazines. "Your secret is safe with me. I won't tell a soul how 'Fabulous' you really are!"

Kate's face had gone red. My jokey dialogue was clearly tanking. But I didn't understand. It had been funny with Ms. Hay and the *Star Trek* novels. What was the difference?

I gave it one more shot.

"I too share a shameful secret," I whispered in an overly dramatic voice.

"Shut up," Kate snapped.

"Oh come on, I'm only joking," I said.

"Shut. Your. Mouth," Kate hissed. Then she pushed roughly past me, actually shoving me to one side.

I stood there for a second, completely stupefied. Was there an instruction manual that came with this girl? Had I somehow missed it? Why did she get bent out of shape over the stupidest things?

I looked around to see if any of the soccer team had overheard the exchange. Impossible to tell. In any case, I must look like an idiot just standing there. I went over to the magazine section as I'd originally planned. I pretended to scan the titles, though I didn't register anything. All I did was play the Kate dialogue over and over in my head.

A quick glance over my shoulder informed me that Kate had made her purchases and was gone. The soccer team was also filing out the door like a single organism composed of many tan legs in knee-socks.

At least I can get my stupid magazine now, I thought.

But once again, there was no *Fabulous* magazine to be had.

Was nothing going to go right?

I approached the checkout lady, too steamed at Kate Southington to be embarrassed about asking after my trashy magazine a second time.

"You're the one that asked about the magazine," she said.

I nodded. "You said—"

"They came in, and they went out. The girl ahead of you bought every copy I had. Sorry."

Kate had bought every copy of *Fabulous* magazine? I was furious. What a petty thing to do. She didn't want me to have my favorite magazine, so she wasted twenty bucks to make sure I couldn't buy one?

But wait. Kate Southington had no way of knowing I loved that magazine. No one at Eaton knew that. She couldn't have known what I was in the bookstore to buy.

So why had she taken the whole stack of copies?

There was definitely something off about the girl. She was acting bizarre. And I *still* felt like I knew her from somewhere. Something was definitely up, and I had to know what it was.

I went straight to the library and grabbed a spare desk in the computer bay. I Googled "Southington" and "Migawam," then "Southington" and "music," but came up empty. Then I Googled "Kate Southington." No hits. I cleared the search field and just reentered "Southington." There were thousands of hits for that. I noticed a link to haveyouheard.com, one of my favorite celebrity gossip sites. I pulled up an archived article flagged "Southington

Family," glanced at the photograph that came up along with it, and drew in a long, deep breath.

It was all right there for the world to see. The picture was of hotel billionaire Lockwood Southington and his two daughters. One of the girls was flaunting herself for the camera, hands on hips, chin slightly lowered, long blond hair hanging in a flawless curtain around her heavily made-up face. She was gorgeous, and she wanted to make sure we all knew she knew it.

The second girl had her face slightly turned away from the camera, head angled down, arms folded over her chest, eyes on the floor. The caption identified the two girls as "aspiring model Brooklyn Stiles Southington and notoriously camera-shy younger sister Phyllida Caytson Southington."

Phyllida. Caytson. Southington.

Caytson Southington.

Kate Southington.

Holy mackerel. This family made celebrity headlines every month! And not in a good way. Brooklyn Southington was the poster girl for trust fund kids—famous for her partying ways, her skimpy outfits, and her rapidly expanding collection of miniature dogs. She drove a neon pink Hummer and had been arrested for various party crimes, like attempting to use a yacht as an impromptu rock arena. Her father was currently awaiting trial for some kind of money-related misbehavior. The mother had run off with a polo player, then returned unrepentant to the family, if memory served. The Southingtons were one of the richest and worst-behaved families in America. When I thought Kate looked familiar, I had no idea how familiar she really was.

And now I knew her secret.

No wonder she had bought every copy of *Fabulous*.

Kate was an Undercover Heiress.

I ran across the quad and into Sage, and jogged up the stairs to the third floor. I was bursting to tell Spinky the secret identity of Kate "All My Cops" Southington.

But by the time I reached my hall, I knew I wasn't going to say anything to Spinky about Kate's secret. As mean as she was, there were just some things a girl didn't do to another girl.

There was only a half hour left of evening study period, and the hall was quiet when I pushed open the glass double doors. Maybe Kristen hadn't done check-in tonight. I paused a moment to catch my breath, then opened the door to our room and hurried inside.

I caught a brief glimpse of something brass colored

wrapped in gauze on the ground as my foot connected with it. I stumbled and pitched forward, landing flat on my face.

Two sets of feet quickly came into view. One wore combat boots.

The other wore suspiciously non-heiress-issue, plain white, brand-spanking-new sneakers.

Chapter Twelve

"**Moxie,** are you concussed?" Spinky said. "I've always wanted to ask someone that," she added.

I looked up to see Kate standing slightly behind Spinky, her arms folded. When our eyes met, she narrowed hers into little slits. Yeah, she hated me. And I was beginning to understand why.

The conversations about how I hated rich people too. The paparazzi comment. The Hummer remark. And at the bookstore—I had told Kate I knew her secret. Did she think I'd been goading her all this time? That I knew her secret and this was my way of telling her? She was probably afraid I would blab. And why wouldn't she be afraid?

Her world was full of ex-friends and disgruntled family employees spilling Southington secrets to the *National Enquirer.* What was I supposed to do? Mouth "Your secret is safe with me"?

"Let me help you up, roomie," Spinky said, extending her hand. I let her pull me up, avoiding eye contact with Kate. "I'm sorry I left the incense thing in the middle of the floor. I've been trying to figure out some kind of sling for it. Except that Kate has pointed out that using gauze will make it a fire hazard."

Kate nodded at Spinky.

"Well, I'm sure you're from a very safety-oriented family," I said. "With all those police and stuff."

I was trying to let her know I was going with her cover story. But my words had the opposite effect. Kate pressed her lips tightly together and her face went white with fury. If Spinky hadn't been standing between us, I feel certain Kate would have ripped my heart right out of my chest.

"Aren't we supposed to stay on our own halls during study period unless we get special permission?" I asked. It sounded rude, but it was the only thing I could think of to get Kate away from me for a while so I could figure out what to do. Because if I told her flat out that I wasn't trying to blow her secret in front of Spinky, all I'd end up doing was, in fact, blowing her secret in front of the only girl at Eaton she seemed to really like.

I decided to give the "I'm sticking with your cover story" thing one more try.

"I get it, though, it's probably really irritating having to hang out in your room. Kate's roommate is this awful trust fund kid," I told Spinky.

"I have a trust fund," Spinky said.

Kate and I both looked at her. I laughed, because I assumed she was joking.

"It's not that big of a deal. It's not billions of dollars or anything. It's from my grandmother. I'm broke at the moment. I don't come into the coin until I'm twenty-one. I think I'll get a Harley."

My face was bright red. I racked my brain trying to remember rude things I'd said about rich people. Had I said any at all, or had I only said those things to Kate? And why had Spinky never mentioned this before? How could Spinky be a DUCKI and a Trust Fund Kid at the same time? The two did not go together. Then again, I'd caught Guadalupe watching *General Hospital* in the TV lounge earlier in the week. How a Hale and Hearty Sports Enthusiast could also be a self-proclaimed soap opera junkie was beyond me.

Spinky shrugged, as if she could read my mind, then bent and picked up the incense burner and began to unravel the gauze sling.

"My grandmother's hilarious. She's eighty-eight and still comes to reunions—she and her mom and my mom all went here."

"Four generations of Spangers?" I asked. She had said something about it, about half the women in her family attending Eaton, but I'd sort of forgotten about it.

"Dempseys and Cornwalls, actually," she said. "I'm the first to go by Spanger—my mom took that name when she married my dad."

"Ah, yes darling, the Dempseys of Dempsey Hall," I joked.

"Yep. Most of the original burned and my great-grand-mother helped pay to fix it, so they named it after her."

I felt my face flush red again. Huge, stone, gargoyles-and-stained-class Dempsey Hall had been paid for by Spinky's family? She said it like her great-grandmother had helped fix a log cabin. Dempsey Hall was much . . . *more*.

"So that sucks that you don't get along with your roommate," Spinky said to Kate.

"She's an idiot, but it has nothing to do with her having

a trust fund, if she even does," Kate said to Spinky. "I think that's Moxie's hang-up."

Spinky appeared to be listening, but she was also turning the brass incense burner over and over in her hands with her head cocked to one side.

Uh ... wait a second. My hang-up? Was she really pinning that on me?

"The problem is always going to be the fire code," Spinky said, hefting the incense burner up and down in her hands. "What we need is a fireman to consult with."

"I was just saying that it wasn't me that ..." Kate's voice trailed off.

"Maybe there's a book on fire codes. Maybe we could Google it," Spinky said.

Spinky was either being deliberately obtuse or she simply hadn't heard what Kate had said. I think we both suspected it was the first. I had noticed that Spinky didn't like conflict of any kind—not even arguing about a band or a flavor of ice cream. She always changed the subject, or agreed with everybody. It was interesting that a girl with green hair who accessorized with safety pins and chains would be constantly avoiding arguments, since she had the appearance of someone who was ready to bring it at a moment's notice.

I shrugged mentally and shook my head. I couldn't think about this. Kate's silent rage was making me highly uncomfortable. There was no way to resolve this situation right now. And if Kate wasn't going to take the hint to go back to her own hall, then I'd just leave myself.

I took the brass incense burner from Spinky's hands.

"I'll run this next door to Haven," I said. "She might as well hang on to it until you come up with your next plan."

"Thanks, roomie," Spinky said. "Tell her I will not give up. I will never surrender!"

"Got it," I said. "See you later, Kate."

Kate bent over to tie a shoelace that wasn't untied, and said nothing.

I walked into the hallway, happy to have an excuse to go into a different room. It was a relief to get away from Kate and the pressures of maintaining my DUCKIness for Spinky under such duress.

Haven's door was open, so I walked a few feet into her room, then stopped.

Haven was sitting on the floor, Buddha style, her hands together with joined thumbs making an O shape in her lap. An electric candle that flickered just like a real (but against the rules) one sat in front of her, placed next to a little Buddha statue and a picture of the happy monk she called her guru. Her eyes were closed, and her face was blank and peaceful.

So this was meditating.

It was such a contrast to the drama I'd just left in my own room. What I wouldn't give to have as peaceful a moment as Haven looked to be having right now. To escape, just for a few minutes, from my personalities and my secret discoveries. Maybe I could even meditate away my mounting terror at the approaching New Student Talent Show. But on second thought, I'm not even sure Buddha himself could meditate away that much anxiety.

I would have continued to stand there watching Haven, but it felt like I was intruding on something private. So I placed the incense burner inside the door and quietly backed out into the hallway. I wandered into the hall lounge for a while, and poked through a selection of discarded magazines that various students had left there. Unfortunately there was no *Fabulous* to be had. When I felt like enough time had passed for Kate to have gone, I went back to my room.

Kate had indeed gone, and Spinky was bustling around in her bedroom.

I suddenly felt exhausted. It had been a long day, I had barely eaten lunch or dinner, and Kate's hostility combined with the huge secret I'd just uncovered had really taken it out of me. I just didn't have the energy to tell Spinky how stressed out I'd gotten over the looming nightmare of the New Student Talent Show. It could wait.

"Spink?" I called. "I think I'm going to hit the hay."

She peered out of her room.

"Me too," she said. "But listen, I got some beta on our roomie. Her name is Dannika Sorenson. She started as an eighth grader last year. Kristen still doesn't know when she's going to show up." Spinky leaned forward. "But listen to this. I heard Dannika was doing an unauthorized experiment in bio last year and there was an explosion that blew out all the lab windows, and all the firemen who came to put it out got chicken pox and nobody could figure out why."

I raised my eyebrows, unsure how to respond to that.

"Apparently she's majorly goth," Spinky continued, "black hair and lipstick, kabuki makeup—the whole nine yards. I will not tolerate any Marilyn Manson posters in my living space, Moxie. Anyway, that's the skinny. I'm knackered. I'm going to try to get up early and work on my poems."

Um, wow. "Night," I said uncertainly, puzzling over this new piece of information. By any of the variety of accounts I'd now heard, the new roommate sounded kind of disastrous. And there was something else. I was surprised the goth thing didn't appeal to Spinky. Nor would I have pegged Spinky as a Marilyn Manson hater. Even more alarmingly, the roommate sounded like she might complicate my already precariously balanced mix of personalities. Was her DUCKI going to outshine mine?

Spinky's green-topped head disappeared as she closed her door. A moment later her light switched out.

In my little room, I changed into a long T-shirt and left everything else in a heap on the floor. I got into bed and pulled the blanket up to my chin. September was almost over, and the nights were already getting pretty cold, but I slept with the window open anyway. After only a few seconds staring at the ceiling, I began to drift into that half-sleep place. My brain switch, however, stayed firmly in the On position.

. . . forgot to call Mom and Dad today! Have to remember to call them before breakfast if there's time . . .

. . . traditional to use a fork or chopsticks with tofu if . . .

. . . what am I going to do about the talent show? What am I going to do?

. . . totally forgot about the Yankees postgame report tonight . . . maybe Guadalupe won't see . . .

. . . why should I even bother explaining to Kate when *she's* the one who . . .

. . . grades too. I'm worried about math, that's always the one that gets me . . . wonder how much the midterm exam counts for? Are we supposed to . . .

. . . going to be at the talent show and they'll find out . . .

. . . but can Buddhists dance?

. . . love that animal rights club, if Reagan could just stop asking about . . .

. . . might as well just let her think I'm going to spill her big secret . . .

. . . if only there wasn't this stupid talent show . . .

. . . going to ruin everything . . .

. . . forgot to tell Spinky about the time my . . .

. . . I wonder if fish can . . .

It went on and on as I tossed and turned, the voices growing louder, arguing with each other, jumping randomly from subject to subject, until I noticed another sound layered on top. I silenced my mind, and I heard a soft, sweet sound in the distance, slightly muffled and wavering, rising and falling, pitch perfect.

Spinky was sleep-singing.

PERSONALITY LOGBOOK—
FOR REFERENCE ONLY

MONDAY
Personality: ARA. Raised my hand in American history when the teacher asked if anyone had ever witnessed an act of civil disobedience, then mysteriously refused to provide any details.

Personality: DUCKI? Told Tashi Hirahato that I had planned on becoming a Green Beret Special Ops team member after high school but a flying woodchip had slightly damaged the peripheral vision in my left eye and I was now forced to rethink my options.

TUESDAY:
Personality: MEG. Sat perfectly still with Haven for 45 minutes and attempted to have no thoughts whatsoever. (Unsuccessful.)

WEDNESDAY:
Personality: DUCKI. Mentioned to the Buckman

twins that I once spent a week at a French seaside in the same villa where Johnny Depp was staying, and I was instrumental in obtaining an eyelash curler for him on the eve of the Deauville Film Festival. I advised the twins that though my French is not good, numerous sources told me he thanked me in his acceptance speech.

Note: Developed a stomachache after the effort of this one and spent the rest of the afternoon in bed.

THURSDAY:

Personality: DUCK! Told the Mavix, captain of the New Student Registration Table, that I was born with extra toes on both feet, but had them surgically removed.

Chapter Thirteen

My Personality Log was beginning to overwhelm me.

In the almost four weeks since I'd started keeping it, there was way too much information piling up. I had actually enjoyed keeping the lists in the beginning, but now just reading over them made me feel queasy. I'd said so many things to so many different people. *I* knew that I was only doing a little harmless personality window-shopping, but on paper my experiment looked . . . not so good. Kind of like the journal entries of a pathological liar.

No one who was not inside my head—meaning everyone—would be able to understand the well-intentioned nature of my storytelling. I was going to have to start eliminating some potential personalities before I made some kind of terrible, cataclysmic blunder. So I decided to give Hale and Hearty Sports Enthusiast one final try. If it didn't feel perfect, I was going to cross it off the list. Forever.

My original plan was to awaken at dawn on Saturday morning, have some MEG time meditating to make a tiny dent in my talent show stress, then assemble a suitable outfit and head down to the sports field to begin stretching. But I had stayed up late the night before, taking advantage of the free evening to hit the practice rooms and begin work on the final section of Variation 28. When I'd gotten to the music wing, though, I'd noticed the concert–length grand piano in the huge choir rehearsal room wasn't being used. I can no more resist a Bosendorfer grand piano than I can a Reese's Peanut Butter Cup. So I propped open the piano's lid to get maximum volume and spent I don't know how many hours thumping out all my favorite sonatas and waltzes while the light fixtures rattled and crystal shattered somewhere in Delaware.

I had gotten back to my room and spent another couple of hours catching up on class reading, including a book of essays by someone named James Thurber that I had to read for EE. When I finally went to bed, I had trouble sleeping. I couldn't stop obsessing over Kate Southington, sea cows, and the New Student Talent Show, and how one—if not all—of them was bound to ruin my life. My stomach, truth be told, had not been okay for several weeks and even my skinny jeans were getting a bit baggy.

Between the stress and the stomach stuff and the lack of sleep, I didn't wake up until nine on Saturday morning. And nothing sporty seemed remotely appealing.

But I was on a quest, and I couldn't write off HHSE until I was certain I'd investigated the possibilities thoroughly.

After grabbing a quick but satisfying breakfast before the dining hall closed, I pulled on a pair of ancient navy sweatpants my mom had tried desperately to get me to throw away, a T-shirt of Spinky's that said "Born to Run" and bore the image of a brown-haired, leather-jacketed geezer who looked like he'd been born to do anything but, and a Minnesota Vikings sweatshirt that I had borrowed from the lost and found. I laced up a pair of white sneakers and capped the look with a purple terrycloth sweatband with a peace sign embroidered on it (purchased over the summer at The Dollar Store). I particularly liked that last bit, since it allowed me to retain a portion of my MEGdom while experimenting with HHSE.

I trotted down the stairs enthusiastically, thrilled when I caught sight of the Mavix in the foyer.

"Hey there!" I called as I skipped past her, pitching my voice a little deeper than usual.

The Mavix looked up at me, then did a double take. I know. I *did* look pretty sharp.

"Just going for a run!" I said loudly, doing the quick-step down the rest of the corridor.

"YankEES!" I yelled. I think she responded, but I didn't hear what she said.

Oh. Guadalupe was the Yankees fan, not the Mavix.

But that's okay! I told myself. I'm an HHSE! Anything sports related goes! And as a zealous fan, I *should* be invading the personal listening space of others with loud verbal displays of support for my team. If Guadalupe was anything to go by, that was simply What One Did.

Sadly, I didn't see anyone else I knew as I trotted across the quad toward the playing field. Nor was there anyone on the field itself, except for one lone figure walking a dog just beyond the far end. I began to question why I was there myself. It was so cold I could see my breath hanging in the air, and there was a frost on the grass. I stamped my feet and blew on my hands, but it didn't really help. I'd better get this over with before I got frostbite.

I'd done my research, and I knew no serious runner

would even think about starting a workout without a proper warm-up. Unfortunately, that was as far as my research had taken me. I did a few things that looked like stretches, but they felt all wrong, which was a good indication they probably looked wrong too.

Then I remembered my mother telling me (repeatedly) that the best all-over body stretch was the yoga position called Downward Facing Dog. Now *that* I could do.

I stretched out on the grass face-down and got myself into a push-up position, wincing at the cold grass between my fingers. Then I pressed up and back, planting my hands in the grass as I straightened my legs, lifted my butt to the clouds, and brought the crown of my head down toward the ground. I hung there in an inverted V—the perfect Downward Facing Dog. I could feel the chi doing whatever it was chi was supposed to do when a yogini practiced her craft.

I heard yelling from a distance behind me, and something that sounded like my name. (One of the few benefits of being named Moxie is there aren't all that many words that sound like it.) I dropped to my knees and stood up, looking around. Way across the quad, three floors up on Sage, two figures were hanging out a window waving and gesturing. One had green hair, the other brown.

Haven and Spinky were cheering me on! I waved at them and did a quick jog in place, flexed a bicep, and waved again before getting back into Downward Facing Dog. Spinky was obviously a running fan—it said so right on the shirt she had lent me. Hopefully Haven could see my peace terrycloth sweatband, and anyway, what was more MEGgy than a little yoga on the fresh green grass?

This feels amazing, I thought. I took the stretch even further, lifting my butt higher and pressing my heels down into the earth. Awesome. I'd been too quick to consider getting rid of my HHSE potential. Why had I neglected my natural gift for athletics for so many years?

As I remained frozen with my head down, watching the upside-down campus through my knees, I saw a small figure walking toward me. From my perspective her feet were clinging to the earth and her head was hanging down into the blue sky. I began to imagine how if gravity let go, she would plummet into the sky never to be seen again, when I recognized her.

It was Ms. Hay.

"Moxie," she was saying, walking kind of quickly toward me. She looked around, like she was checking to make sure no one else was there.

"Moxie, hi," came her voice.

I stubbornly remained in Downward Facing Dog. I greeted her, but upside down it came out more like *huwuhay*.

"Nice Downward Façing Dog," Ms. Hay said. "But if I could interrupt you a moment—"

I interrupted her instead, with the sound of my body collapsing and smacking onto the grass. It was harder to stay in that position that I thought.

"Are you okay?"

"Yeph," I said, my voice muffled by the grass I'd planted my face in.

"Oh, good. I don't want to embarrass you, but I really need to tell you something, Moxie . . ."

All of a sudden my so-called Amish life came back to me in a rush. She knew the truth! I got to my feet, poised to escape.

"Sorry, I'm on a schedule," I said, pointing at the field, but Ms. Hay was undeterred. She was wearing jeans that looked so new, they had a crease down the front, with a good three inches of cuff rolled up. Her shirt had short puffed sleeves, tiny flowers, and a bow at the neckline. Yikes.

"Vikings fan, huh?" she asked.

I stared down at my sweatshirt.

"Well, they're okay. But my team is the Yankees. They're

going to cream the Vikings this season!" I growled with gusto.

Ms. Hay paused.

"I'm not sure that's possible," she said.

"Forget the odds, forget what you read in the papers," I said, mimicking something Guadalupe had said to me. "Read my lips: Yankees—World Series—this year. No Vikings are going to stand in their way."

Ms. Hay nodded, a small smile on her lips.

"I'd have to agree, given that the Vikings are a football team," she said.

Crud.

"Well, yeah. There's that too, of course. That James Thurber book was pretty funny. What else has he written?" I maintained an innocent face during the rapid subject change I had initiated.

Ms. Hay moved closer to me.

"Moxie," she said very quietly. "Listen—I couldn't help noticing that your—"

"Actually, sorry, but I'm starting to lose the heat from that stretch," I said hastily. Because I was pretty sure where she was going with her quiet, seemingly urgent advice. "Gotta run before my muscles cool down."

I took off, running faster than I'd planned to.

Was it against school rules to refuse to allow a teacher to finish a sentence if that conversation took place outside of class? What was I running for, anyway? She was still going to know about the Amish thing when I stopped running. The question was, what was she planning on doing about it?

I kept running.

She was still standing there when I completed my first lap around the field. I could see her lips were moving and her brow was furrowed as I ran by, but I put my head down and ran faster. When I reached the far end of the field, I noticed she'd been joined by the Dean of Students, Mr. Werner, and his famous offspring, Luscious Luke. Luscious Luke looked particularly flawless this morning in a crimson fleece and faded jeans. His flaxen hair looked lightly tousled and was doing some outstanding flopping over one eyebrow. How was I supposed to jog realistically while he was standing there? As Dean Werner was talking, Ms. Hay glanced in my direction, then took the dean by the arm and guided him toward the quad in the direction of the administration buildings. Luscious Luke trailed behind.

This was much worse than I thought. Ms. Hay was talking to the dean. At this very moment I was probably being reported for False Representation of Religionality. Was this an expellable offense? How could I have ever thought it was okay to make something up to a teacher?

Now that no one was watching, I stopped running, and stood on the field gasping for breath.

I'm going to be expelled, I thought. I am totally going to be expelled!

What had I been thinking? Sea cows and sports teams and rumpspringers and Wicca . . . It was too much for any one person to keep straight, even with a Personality Log. Ms. Hay was clearly onto me. What if *everyone* was onto me?

Ms. Hay, the dean, and Luscious Luke had disappeared into Dempsey Hall. I headed for Sage. Should I call my parents now? Was the dean already calling them? I felt like hyperventilating.

Students were filing in and out of the dining hall when I reached the Sage lobby. Everyone seemed unusually cheerful. Loud laughter echoed through the halls, a sharp contrast to Auntie Sparkles's severe gaze. I ignored everyone and sped up the stairs.

When I reached my room, Haven was still there with Spinky, and their concern was clear on both their faces.

Uh-oh.

"Are you okay? That didn't look good," Spinky said gently.

I knew it. I was in trouble.

"Ms. Hay came out to the playing field," I said, my voice a bit wobbly. "And so did the Dean of Students."

"And Luscious Luke," Spinky said. "I'm really sorry, Mox. I felt your pain."

So it was true. I had been kicked out of Eaton for impersonating the Amish.

"How did you hear about it so fast?" I asked, tears coming to my eyes.

"Hear about it?" Haven asked. She took my hand, and squeezed it. "We saw it with our own eyes. It was like that movie that came out last year—*The Beast of Bottomless Lake*—the one in 3D." She looked from me to Spinky. "Did no one see that movie?"

I was too traumatized by my own tragedy to respond to Haven's perplexing film reference. What was a Buddhist doing watching *The Beast of Bottomless Lake*?

"We tried to warn you," Spinky said. "Didn't you hear us yelling from the window?"

"No," I said, a tear spilling down my cheek. "I thought you were cheering for me. Anyway, what difference would it have made?"

"Well, you could have changed into another pair of sweatpants, for starters," Spinky said gently.

I looked from Spinky to Haven, confused. Haven was looking at my butt, though she averted her eyes quickly.

Wait a minute.

I reached back and swatted my hand in the vicinity of my backside. Where there should have been sweatpant material, there was only . . . air.

I rushed over to the mirror, turned my back to it, then craned my neck to look over my shoulder.

The seam of the material had given way, forming a rip that was a good eight inches long, creating a lighting-bolt-shaped window framing a section of my extremely orange underpants.

Like people I've seen interviewed about near-death experiences, a rapid montage of scenes flashed before my eyes. The Mavix doing a double take. Me trotting across the quad with a rip in my pants so large it was probably visible from space. And oh, no, Ms. Hay finding me in Downward Facing Dog . . . and Luscious Luke . . . How could I ever survive the humiliation?

Wait, though. Wait. This changed everything. Ms. Hay had not come to expel me. She had come over to warn me that my underwear was glowing like a beacon in front of the whole campus. And when Mr. Werner and Luscious Luke showed up, she had tactfully led them in another direction. Oh man, I was such a moron! I should have dropped the Hearty Hill Sports Confusiast weeks ago!

I took a breath. I was a moron, yes. But I wasn't expelled.

I made a sound that was somewhere between a gasp, a sob, and a cry of relief. Ms. Hay had been trying to help me out, girl to girl, even after I had made up a story to get out of the talent show. I would never claim to be sporty or Amish again. I would cross that personality off the list immediately. And I needed to do some serious housecleaning on the rest of the personalities. Could I tell Guadalupe I was giving up the Yankees for Lent? When *was* Lent? Might I convince the Buckman twins that my Johnny Depp story was actually a working exercise in Self-Confidence Through Comedy, as opposed to actual fact? Oh no, had I eaten BACON this morning?!! Who had been at breakfast? *Who had seen me?*

Spinky put her arm around my shoulder as I tried to catch my breath.

"Well," she said, after a moment. "Orange you glad you wore underwear?"

PERSONALITY LOGBOOK—
FOR REFERENCE ONLY

Friday
Personality: DUCKI. Advised American history
class that I had been asked to play a drum
solo on the upcoming album of a punk/metal
fusion band so hot and exclusive, I was not
at liberty to divulge their name.

Saturday
Personality: MEG. Told sophomore with long
braids that I weave and dye my own cloth
from hemp and organic cotton and offered to
sew her an all-natural caftan.

Sunday
Personality: ARA. Confronted lunch lady and
loudly and publicly demanded written proof that
the seafood salad contained only dolphin-safe
tuna and farm exclusive rehabilitated shrimp
(note to self: probably no such thing as farm
exclusive rehabilitated shrimp).

EXTREMELY IMPORTANT NOTE:
HHSE personality no longer under
consideration by this individual!

Chapter Fourteen

It took days and days for me to recover from my failed HHSE experience. It wasn't so much the embarrassment stemming from my sweatpants malfunction with Luscious Luke so nearby, although that was excruciating, but the recollection of the way I'd felt when I thought I'd been busted. Granted, I'd only thought I'd been caught for about ten minutes before Spinky enlightened me, but the feeling of dread was still very fresh.

More and more, I tried to turn my thoughts to how to get myself out of the hole I'd been digging since arriving at Eaton. I thought of all the lucky, lucky people who get abducted by UFOs and whisked away to other planets. Why couldn't that happen to me? Probably because aliens were telepathic and knew all about my personality-creation-disorder. My story was like a low-budget indie film nobody would go to see—*Moxie Roosevelt: Even the Aliens Didn't Want Her.*

Algebra plus Kate plus my EE talent show requirement had been enough to flip me out. But now there was more. And to think, my piano lesson had started out so nicely.

"It seems crazy, and it takes up huge amounts of time, but I'm finding if I try playing all thirty variations straight through, it helps me make progress on Variation 28. Somehow tackling the whole thing helps me to get each part of it, if that makes any sense," I told Mr. Tate.

He grabbed his white mop of hair with both hands, then shot his arms in the air.

"Miss Kippah, you have excessively good intuition. And you work harder than a bee in a sugar field. You will not be the least bit surprised, I suspect, when I tell you I can hear it. I hear it, Miss Kippah—the work you put in is clear as the summer sun in every note you play."

I glowed. Beams of light were probably shooting out of my eyes. I loved that my hours of practice time were paying off in Mr. Tate's view. Imaginary bluebirds soared merrily around my head. And then it happened.

"Miss Kippah, would you be interested in representing the music department in the New Student Talent Show?" Mr. Tate asked.

I would be more interested in hanging from Sage Tower by my hair while singing the entire score of *Lion King*.

"Definitely!" I lied brightly.

Mr. Tate rubbed his beard happily.

"I thought you'd say so. I'll leave the choice of what piece you'd like to perform to you, Miss Kippah. I know you'll pick something worthy of you."

I gave Mr. Tate my biggest smile, but in truth I didn't feel so good. I willed myself to keep it together. I had never thrown up at the piano, and I wasn't about to start now.

Now I was performing *twice* at the New Student Talent Show? Musical Moxie had to mix with Not So Comical Moxie? How was that ever going to work? If only this was all I had to deal with. But I had other things on my mind too—a growing list of problems crowned by a brand-new Unfortunate Encounter with Kate Southington. The list went something like this:

1. The New Student Talent Show was just over one week away.
2. I really wanted to go for Variation 28 to show Mr. Tate I

was worthy of him. But what if my attempt at the new piece inspired more laughs than my comedy?

3. I was not doing so well in math. Not so well at *all*.

4. The New Student Talent Show was just over one week away!

5. I had launched into a passionate endorsement of soy-based meat substitutes with a sophomore that I thought was a MEG from Mystic, Connecticut, with a Grateful Dead collection on vinyl. After she called me a "tree-hugging nut loaf" and walked away, a peek into my Personality Log revealed she was actually a softball fanatic from Tennessee whose father owned the South's largest sausage-processing plant. Zounds. What other details was I blundering?

6. The New Student Talent Show was just over *one week away!!!*

7. Luscious Luke waved to me at the lunch buffet while PEELING AN ORANGE, which was clearly a passive-aggressive taunt indicating that in spite of Ms. Hay's best efforts, he was aware of my Sweatpants Malfunction.

8. A seventh grader from my old school was supposedly considering coming up for an Eaton tour, which created so many potential complications for all of the mess I'd created, I had lost three pounds in two days.

9. The New Student Talent Show was just over ONE WEEK AWAY!!!%#!
10. There was the tiniest miniature possibility I had temporarily misplaced my Personality Log.

Yeah, I saved the worst for last. There was no two ways around it. I could not find my Personality Log. I figured there were three possibilities. It was lost in plain sight in my room, and I'd find it at some point even though I'd torn the place apart twice already. Or, I had dropped it somewhere where no one would ever find or notice it, hopefully down a storm drain, and that would be that. Or, I had left it where someone had and would find it, open it, and read it. I was not ready to fully process what that could mean for me. Only that it would be the end of Moxie Roosevelt as Eaton knew her. As Eaton knew all of the different hers.

That is, if Kate Southington wasn't the end of me first.

The latest Unfortunate and Unsettling Encounter with Kate had been over practically before it started, but it had rattled me, largely because I was already freaked about the loss of my log, and I had no idea what the encounter really meant. It took place at breakfast check-in, when Kate and I happened to be reporting our presence to the housemother on duty at the same time.

"Southington," Kate had announced crisply to the housemother.

"Yes. And Moxie Roosevelt Kipper?" the housemother had asked, her pen poised next to my name on her clipboard.

"The one and only," I declared, a little too loudly and cheerfully because Kate standing next to me made me nervous.

I thought she would speed away from me as we left the housemother's table, because she always made a point of getting away from me as quickly as possible. But this time she matched my walk, and when I glanced over at her I was surprised to see an ugly sneer on her face.

"The one and only," she said, imitating me in a mocking voice. "The one and only Moxie Roosevelt. What a stupid name. You know it's a big joke in this school, right? People laugh at you. Everybody does. I almost feel sorry for you."

"What are you talking about?" My voice came out in a croak.

"You know exactly what I mean. And you know what? I'm not going to tolerate it anymore."

Then she *did* speed off, practically sprinting out the dining hall door.

I was horrified by the whole encounter, and especially freaked out by her last words. She wasn't going to tolerate *what* anymore?

Wasn't going to tolerate *what*?

"Moxie, did you hear me? You look like you're on another planet!"

I looked up at Ms. Hay, genuinely startled. "I'm sorry, can you repeat the question?"

"I asked if you thought P. G. Wodehouse's humor holds up in present-day culture. Did the Jeeves and Bertie stories make you laugh?"

I nodded, still unable to really focus on Ms. Hay, my brain still rehashing the events of the morning. My stomach ached terribly, and my heart was pounding. I felt like I was going to throw up. I started to get a terrible feeling that the thing with Kate and the disappearance of my Personality Log were in some way connected.

That's ridiculous, I told myself firmly. It was bound to show up. I probably really had misplaced it somewhere in the mess of my room. As soon as EE was over, I'd tear the room apart a third time, and I would find the book. But between Kate and not knowing exactly where the log was, I was practically having a full-blown panic attack.

What had I been thinking? The personality experiment

in and of itself was bad enough. The log was a smoking gun—written proof of all the stories I'd made up, and who I'd told them to. Nobody who did not know me well could possibly understand why I'd done it. I had to find that book and get rid of it. It was time to start setting things right. I thought of the sausage-making-family sophomore who'd gotten mad at me when I mistakenly thought she'd appreciate my vegetarian talk. That had not felt good at all. Far worse was Reagan offering her steadfast friendship, so relieved I wasn't one of the "fakers" she thought Eaton would be full of. What would Reagan think of me if she read what was in that log? What would Haven or Spinky think? Not to mention the others, girls whose last names I didn't even know, like Guadalupe the Yankees fan, and Charnay from South Africa who was going to be a writer . . . Tashi and the Mavix and Dellarose from Philly who thought I could tango. So many people. So many personalities. And what had it all gotten me? I didn't have an exciting new personality at all. I was on the verge of being nothing but a fraud and a failure!

I had to call it off. Not just the Personality Log, but all of it. The whole Reinvention of Moxie Roosevelt had to be abandoned, and somehow I had to find a way to come clean, especially with Spinky, Haven, and Reagan. If I was going to get by at this school with real friends, if I was going to deal with people like Kate, I had to be regular old me, I realized with twin pangs of misery and relief. I needed to go over my personality trail with an industrial-sized vacuum cleaner before my life exploded and created a mess so gigantic that nothing could fix it.

". . . novels of this era, because the things we find funny in them are . . . Moxie?"

"Yes, I do," I said automatically.

The silence that followed jolted me back to reality.

Ms. Hay was standing in front of the large desk by the blackboard, leaning against it.

"Are you feeling okay, Moxie?" she asked. She watched me closely.

"Yes," I said, but then I shook my head.

"No?" she asked. Her voice was very quiet and compassionate.

"No," I said softly. A tear rolled down my cheek before I could pretend that my eye was just itchy—or Amish—and needed rubbing.

"Moxie, you can trust me," Ms. Hay said. "This is only EE, it's just a pass/fail thing for credit. It's not that big of a deal. But if something's really bothering you, that *is* a big deal. You might feel a lot better if you just talked about it."

I'm sure she was right. But where did I begin? That I had come to school to reinvent myself? That I had gotten a little bogged down in a number of different personalities that had turned me into a sideshow act—The Girl with a Hundred Faces? That I had unwittingly discovered an Undercover Heiress and had kept her secret even in spite of the fact that the girl was constantly horrible to me? How could I have been so stupid to think a person could reinvent themselves like this? It was insane!

"I'm not Amish," I said, my head hanging low.

After a moment, I peeked up at Ms. Hay. She was clasping her little hands in front of her chest, a small smile on her face.

"I know that, Moxie," she said.

"You do?" I said, catching my breath. Then I did a little hiccuppy thing and started blubbering for real.

Ms. Hay was the nicest teacher at Eaton, and in her own odd way, one of the most awesome people I knew. And I'd lied to her for a stupid reason, and I felt terrible about that. And still, she was being nice to me.

"I do. I knew the first day you said it that you weren't Amish," she said.

I blubbered a bit more, and through my tears mouthed, "How?"

Ms. Hay walked over to my desk and knelt down next to me.

"I knew you weren't, Moxie, because I *am* Amish. You messed up on the secret handshake."

My mouth dropped open in horror.

Oh no! Not only had I lied, I had insulted Ms. Hay's religious freedom!

"You're . . . Amish?" I whispered.

Ms. Hay gave me one of her wide hobbit grins.

"Nope. That was a *joke*, sweetie. Have you been paying attention at all in this class?"

I thought I was going to start sobbing again, but instead a different sound came out of me—the half-cry, half-laugh sound that has no name. It became all laugh as I wiped my eyes.

"That day on the playing fields," I said, "I ran off because I thought you had come to confront me about the Amish thing. And when the dean showed up, I was sure I was being expelled."

Ms. Hay changed her position from kneeling to sitting on the floor by my desk, and stretched her legs out in front of her.

"So that's why you took off like that. I was just trying to tell you that—"

I smacked my forehead. "My sweatpants were ripped, I know," I said. "Orange underwear."

"Yep," Ms. Hay said.

"Talk about being the butt of the joke," I said glumly.

Ms. Hay snorted, then made a sound more like a cackle than a laugh. She smacked one little hand on her knee. "Eureka!" she shouted.

"What?"

She jabbed a finger in the air, gesturing at me.

"You just dealt with an embarrassing situation by making a joke out of it, Moxie," Ms. Hay said.

Hey. She was right. I *had*.

"Which is the point of this entire EE. You are so passing this class."

"I am? I'm passing?"

"*So* passing," Ms. Hay repeated, looking supremely satisfied.

"So I don't have to do the New Student Talent Show?"

She grinned. "Nice try. You *do* have to do the New Student Talent Show, and I can't wait to see what you've come up with."

Crud.

"And since we still have about fifteen minutes of class time left, what do you say you bite the bullet and tell me the whole story behind your suddenly becoming Amish on the first day of EE?"

I sighed, a smile still on my face. The thread was already beginning to unravel, so what did I have to lose by confiding the secret of my reinvention to Ms. Hay?

I took a deep breath.

"Okay. Do you ever wonder what goes through some people's heads when they come up with names for their kids? Take my name, for example."

And as Ms. Hay got more comfortable on the floor, I told her the whole story from the very beginning.

Chapter Fifteen

So that was a good thing. I had unburdened myself, and now there was one person at Eaton who knew the whole truth about me. Ms. Hay hadn't chimed in with any advice or an opinion. She had just listened to what I had to say, and nodded. And that was that. She had actually seen the real me, and the world had not ended. My list of problems was still hefty. Kate still loathed and despised me. Any number of things might suddenly blow up in my face. And I wasn't at all ready to perform Variation 28 in less than a week. But I felt like Ms. Hay had my back now. Which was weird, but good. Things were straight between us.

I had to do the same thing with Spinky and Reagan and

Haven. Just fess up and get things straight with them. If I was very honest, and very lucky, maybe it would all unfold pretty much the same as it had with Ms. Hay. I'd tell them how I'd wanted to reinvent myself, and how it had started spinning out of control. We'd laugh about it. It would all be out in the open.

Yep. I had to come clean with my friends.

But not just yet.

I had to keep juggling my personalities for just a little while longer. Just until I found the Personality Log and got rid of it. It was the final loose end that needed to be tied up. I had to make sure that my personality experiment was explained to my friends, in my own words. That way I could make them see that I'd meant well the whole time—that it wasn't the pointless pack of lies that it looked like on paper. Because the time was now—I had to decide once and for all who I was going to be.

And there was something else I wanted to do too.

In spite of her sneering and her mocking and her "I'm not going to tolerate this," I needed to let Kate know that regardless of what she thought, I was not holding her secret over her head.

In spite of the hurt Kate had caused me, telling me I was nothing more than a huge joke to the school, part of me knew that only a miserable person will lash out unprovoked at someone like that.

I knew in my heart Kate was a bitter, unhappy girl.

And part of my making up for my personality deception had to be to reach out to her. After all, who better than I could understand why a person might want to pretend to be someone they were not? I was practically the Ambassador to Fictionalized-Character-Land. And in all likelihood Kate really only hated me because I knew the truth about who she was. I had to be like a Ms. Hay for Kate. I'd help her get things straight with one person at Eaton. Then she'd see that everything was okay.

I had to do all of those things, just as soon as I found that Personality Log and tore it to pieces before anyone read it without my explaining it to them.

Except when I got back to my room, I searched every crevice for my Personality Log for over an hour.

I couldn't find it anywhere.

I held out hope the rest of the week. Every time my schedule took me someplace I hadn't been for several days, I took the opportunity to search. I searched the bio lab. The library. The lost and found by the admissions office. The gym locker room. And every time my search came up empty, I thought of Kate. But she had been steering well clear of me all week. If she by some crazy chance had gotten my Personality Log, she certainly would have done something about it by now. Right? I'd just have to keep looking.

I dealt with the stress of the missing Personality Log by avoiding as many people as I could. I holed myself up in my practice room and obsessively played Variation 28—badly, I thought. But just working at it, working at anything, made me feel better. I holed myself up in my bedroom, trying to do algebra—also badly, which did *not* make me feel better. I knew if I talked to people, though, I'd probably end up adding facts to my personalities and getting myself in deeper just when I was ready to get out.

So when Reagan came by to talk about starting her club, I pretended to be asleep. When Haven invited me to come watch *The Haunting of Gothic Manor* on TV, I was momentarily caught off guard. Her unexpectedly robust appetite for B-horror-movies made me curious. But then I remembered my situation, and told her I had too much homework. When Spinky offered to take me to Jumble Thrift Gems to revitalize my wardrobe, I told her I'd spent my allowance already. Midterm exams were coming up, so everyone was lying low a little bit. I just lay lower than most.

But not completely out of sight. I ran into Reagan in

the afternoon when I was leaving the phone room and she was going in.

"Mox!" she exclaimed, grabbing my arms and looking so pleased to see me, I almost backed out of her reach from sheer guilt. "So I've got a date!"

"A date?" I asked her. "With a boy?"

I had an absurd flash of Reagan holding hands with Luscious Luke.

"With the dean," Reagan corrected. "Moxie, hello? What have I been living and breathing for weeks?"

"Oh, the appointment to pitch your club!" I exclaimed. How could I have forgotten about that? It only meant the entire world to Reagan.

"And I have this great idea. Do you want to come along? I was thinking you could talk about the sloop, and the sea cow. You know, not that many people know about the sea cow. I think it could really have an impact if I show up with another student—somebody like you—who is already serious and committed about animal rights. Somebody who's already shown that she's willing to devote time and energy like you did on the sloop this summer."

Oh no. No no no.

Reagan wanted me to walk into the office of the person ultimately in charge of all discipline issues at Eaton, and lie through my teeth to him—and to her. Again! I couldn't do it.

"Oh Reagan, I really can't. I'm sorry."

"Oh."

Her face fell.

"I'm really, really sorry. I just . . . It's complicated. I can't talk to the dean. Not right now. I can't . . . talk about it yet."

Reagan's eyes met mine. She looked at me carefully, and an expression of concern crossed her face.

"Is something wrong? Are you okay?"

I nodded. "I am. I will be. Like I said, it's just . . . complicated."

Reagan held my gaze.

"Moxie, you know you can tell me anything, right?"

I nodded again.

Tell her. *Tell her now.*

But no. I was determined to get the log back first. I'd give it one more day. If it still didn't turn up, I'd confess. Reagan would be the first person I went to.

"It's fine, Reagan. Seriously."

She let it go, and she let me go, and I went upstairs feeling as small as a dwarf lima bean. I redoubled my efforts to find the Personality Log. And I felt I actually, *finally* knew where it might be. I had chosen a photographer named Margaret Bourke-White for my midterm history project, and I'd taken out a bunch of books on her from the library. When Charnay came knocking to ask if she could borrow them, I lent her the whole stack. Now I realized that I had to have accidentally included the Personality Log in the pile. All I had to do was find Charnay, and get the books back.

The only things that kept me from completely falling apart worrying about all this stuff—the log, the talent show, the Kate thing, *everything*—were the meditation lessons I'd gotten from Haven, and the fact that I now had Ms. Hay to talk to. She was my Oprah. I poured it all out to her every time we got together, with no pauses for commercial interruptions. Sometimes we spent more time talking about The Reinvention of Moxie Roosevelt than we did about comedy. She didn't offer any theory about Kate. She never told me what to do at all—she just listened. But when I said that I planned to junk the whole personality experiment and explain to my friends what I'd been doing, she nodded vigorously.

"Yeah, I agree with you, Moxie. That's a good idea, and the sooner, the better."

We were sitting at adjoining desks leaning toward each other like two freshmen passing notes. The comedy essay she had photocopied for me to read lay ignored on my desk.

"I've just got to find the Personality Log first. So I can rip it up and throw it away and no one will ever see it. I want to explain things to people on my terms, without worrying that the book will show up to haunt me."

Ms. Hay looked thoughtful.

"And that needs to happen before you talk to your friends?"

I nodded. "But I did make some progress this morning. I left a note for Kate, saying we needed to talk as soon as possible. I've been thinking about it, and I've realized I need to take action and try to make peace with her. Because I'm pretty sure she's been thinking all this time I was holding her secret over her head, but I wasn't. She'll see it's all okay when I explain it to her. See, 'cause I've learned my lesson about all this, so I have to be the bigger person with her now, and . . . what do they call it? Pay it forward to Kate, or whatever. That sounded lame, but you know what I mean."

"Hmmm," Ms. Hay said, her tiny lips pressed together.

"What?"

"I just think you need to be careful," she said.

"Oh, no. Of course. I'll be careful," I said.

I guess Ms. Hay thought I might give in to the temptation to gloat a bit to Kate after she realized I knew who she really was. But Ms. Hay would see. I had seriously learned my lesson. I would not be smug while Kate learned hers.

"Maybe we should talk about this Steve Martin piece. Since you were supposed to have read it."

"Sure, sure," I said. "And I did read it. He's funnier on TV."

"And I'm supposed to be following up with you on your

prep for the New Student Talent Show," Ms. Hay added. "We only have a few days left."

I squirmed. Honesty was my new policy with Ms. Hay, but the truth was I hadn't done any work on preparing at all. I'd done plenty of inner belly-aching and freaking out, but no actual writing.

"Is it required that I figure it out by a certain date?" I asked.

She gave me a scrutinizing glance.

"No," she said slowly. "But I highly recommend you not leave it till the last minute. Which is almost here already."

"Oh no," I said. "Not to the last minute. See, that's the thing about me, Ms. Hay—I always do what I say I'm going to do, eventually. I'll be ready for the talent show."

"At the risk of sounding very boring and very ancient, Moxie, there's an old saying that goes 'Never put off till tomorrow what you can do today.' Something you might want to keep in mind."

I beamed at my teacher.

"I will," I said.

And I meant it. I intended to.

But it was already too late.

Chapter Sixteen

I was actually in a really good mood after EE, and I hurried back to my room, full of plans about how I would go to Kate and we would talk and fix all our misunderstandings. But as soon as I opened the door to my suite, I saw that something was very wrong. There were a bunch of people there. People I knew. Haven. Reagan. Sage was there, and Guadalupe, and the Mavix. And standing closest to the door was Kate Southington, who was looking at me through narrowed eyes.

"And speak of the devil, here she is now," said Kate. "Why don't we just ask her to explain it to us herself?"

I looked around at the faces in the room, confused. What

were all these people doing in my room, and where was Spinky? Haven gave me a small smile, but Reagan looked very upset, and the triumphant expression on Kate's face was making me very nervous.

"Go on, explain," Kate said. "Maybe this will help jog your memory."

She tossed something toward me, and by reflex I caught it.

It was my Personality Log. I had not lost it. Kate had stolen it from me.

"That's my . . . book," I said flatly, looking only at Kate. So I had left the book in my room then. "You came into my room and took this?"

"Oh, so I'm the criminal now? Give me a break. I read all your little lists, Moxie, if that's even your real name."

"It *is* my real name." Who in the known universe would invent such a name?

"If you say so, *Moxie*. You're quite the identity thief. So I took the liberty of tracking down some of your victims. I think you owe them all an explanation."

My face was burning as I locked eyes with Kate. How dare she, of all people, call me out on things I'd made up about myself? And not even in private. She had bided her time going through the lists of lies I'd told, and gathered the people I'd told them to in my own room! My stomach lurched. I felt like throwing up. I was the one who knew *her* secret! Didn't she realize I could just blurt her true identity out to everyone right now? Or did she think my credibility would be so damaged no one would ever believe anything I said again?

"Can we speed this along, people?" asked the Mavix. "I've got an extra-help trig session scheduled that I can't be late for."

"Fine," Kate said. She pointed at the Mavix. "She told you she had extra toes."

"Oh please, this is about toes? You underclassmen don't know the meaning of the words *academic pressure*. You kids figure this out yourself."

She was out of the room in a flash, but Kate looked undaunted. She pointed at Guadalupe.

"She told you she was a Yankees fan," Kate declared.

Guadalupe looked from Kate to me, frowning.

"You're not a Yankees fan?" she asked.

"They're fine," I mumbled.

"She doesn't know anything about them," Kate said. "She made it all up. She was making fun of you."

"I wasn't making fun of anyone!" I protested. My voice sounded thin and weird. My face felt funny, and my head seemed huge, like one of those aliens from Roswell. Where was Spinky?

"But that's . . . why would anyone do that? What's your problem?"

"I don't have a—I just wanted to . . . I'm sorry, Lupe. The Yankees really seem very interesting."

Guadalupe put her hand up.

"Save it. Seriously, *mira*, you know what? The Yankees are the greatest ball team in the world. They're not hurting for fans. I don't appreciate the charade, okay? But I'm definitely not interested in the little drama you've got going on here. I missed the first half hour of *General Hospital* for this, and enough is enough. So whatever your deal is Moxie, and whatever your deal is, Kate, leave me out of it."

"What's this? A party?"

Finally. Spinky had appeared in the doorway. Only now I wished she'd stayed away.

"Not a party," Lupe said, pushing past Spinky. "I'm out of here."

"It's enough now, Kate," Haven said. "Stop it."

"What's going on?" Spinky asked. The smile left her face as she looked around. "Did someone get kicked out?"

"Your roommate has been lying to everybody, and keeping notes in a book so she'd get her stories straight.

Here, look at it." Kate grabbed the book from me and thrust it toward Spinky. Spinky looked at her, but made no move to take it.

"That's enough," Haven said, louder.

"She's not a Wiccan. She didn't even know what one—"

"I don't care! Stop it!" Haven shouted.

Everyone gaped at her. I don't think any of us knew she could shout.

"I care," said Reagan.

She looked really angry. And she wasn't making eye contact with me.

"Reagan, listen," I said anxiously. "I actually am incredibly—"

"There *is* no sea cow group that owns a sloop," Reagan said. "You made the whole thing up."

I took a deep breath.

"I did make that part up, Reagan, and I'm sorry. But I really do—"

"There isn't even a sea cow to be endangered!" Reagan yelled.

My mouth dropped open.

"I—"

"Do you know why? Because it's ALREADY extinct. I finally looked it up this morning, Moxie, because I was going to be stupid enough to tell the dean about it myself. The North Atlantic sea cow was discovered in the 1740s, and less than thirty years later humans had hunted it to extinction. Hunted the entire species to extinction!"

How could that be? I had *invented* the sea cow. Or so I'd thought. I half laughed in disbelief. I was an environmental psychic.

"You might find that funny, but it isn't a *joke* to me!" Reagan cried.

"No, I didn't . . . of course it's not a joke. Reagan, the amazing thing is I didn't even—"

"Everybody in this room is just a lab rat to Moxie," Kate said.

"No, no, it isn't like that at all!" I said wildly. "Reagan, listen. I didn't do it as a joke. I just wanted to get your attention. I was trying to *be* like you."

Reagan was shaking her head, and I could see she had tears in her eyes.

"You are *nothing* like me," she said.

"I was going to tell you. And Haven, and Guadalupe, and everyone. I was going to explain it all."

"Then why didn't you? I asked you if there was something wrong. I told you that you could tell me anything," Reagan reminded me coldly.

"Because I was waiting until I found my . . ."

There was no point. Ms. Hay was right—I never should have put it off. What difference did it make whether I had the stupid Personality Log back or not? That wasn't a reason, it was a delay tactic. I'd been putting off the unpleasant task of fessing up. I wanted to do it totally on my terms, in my way. I wanted to control the way the truth unfolded. Now it was too late.

"I was being a coward about it, Reagan. There's really nothing else to it."

Reagan stared at me, then nodded.

"Yeah," she said. "I've gotta be someplace."

She brushed past me, followed by Sage, who gave me a puzzled look as she walked past me and out the door.

I turned to Spinky, who was looking at me, her eyebrows furrowed.

"I've never been in trouble," I said. "I came to boarding school because I got a music scholarship and there's no high school in my town. I never planned on getting a tattoo. I'm not detached, or cool, or unique. I've never even heard a Frank Zappa song. I wanted to be like you, Spinky. I wanted to be like Haven, and I wanted to be like Reagan. I wanted to be everybody but me, and I made up stories, and I'm sorry, Spinky, I'm really, really sorry . . ."

Spinky came over to me and put her arms around my shoulders.

"I have no idea what's going on," she said in my ear. "But you're my friend. Just sit tight."

"Look, there's other stuff in here about you," Kate said. "You need to read it, Spinky."

Spinky fixed Kate with a long look.

"No, I don't think I do," she said. "I think I've heard enough. I don't want any fighting going on—especially in my own room. I don't care who did what, period. I've got plenty of flaws, but I don't talk trash about people, and I don't judge. That's me. I already told you that, Kate."

"*She* had no problem telling you things about me that were none of her business," Kate said. She folded her arms over her chest, but the look she gave Spinky was almost pleading. *She wants to be Spinky*, I thought. *That's the thing.*

"Telling me what about you? Moxie's never told me anything about you," Spinky said.

"About my family," Kate said. She glanced quickly at Haven, the only other person in the room, and ducked her head.

"Kate, I honestly don't know what you're talking about. Moxie hasn't told me anything about your family, or anything else relating to you that I can remember."

Kate looked flabbergasted. Which was how I felt. *That*

was why Kate had done this? Because she thought I'd told Spinky who she was?

"I've never said anything to anybody about your family, Kate," I said, glaring. And the impulse to reveal who they were now had never been more overpowering. But still I didn't.

"Say what you want, but it's all right there in the note you left me," Kate muttered. "You told, you were about to tell, what's the difference?"

What was all right there? All the stupid note said was that we needed to talk right away. How deluded was Kate to turn that into a threat?

"Tell what?" asked Haven.

I shook my head. It would be so easy to do it now. Nobody would blame me for blabbing a secret that sooner or later the whole school was going to find out about anyway. Kate was an idiot if she thought she could keep her identity hidden for long. I ought to know.

"There's nothing to tell," I said, gritting my teeth.

Kate glared at me. She was going to hate me no matter what I did. Whether I blabbed, or kept my mouth shut, she'd find a way to justify despising me. She was going to decide my note had been threatening no matter what it had actually said.

"People, I don't do conflict," Spinky said.

"Neither do I," Haven piped up.

"That's the dumbest thing I've ever heard," Kate said. "Everyone does conflict. Conflict is a part of life. You either face it, or you're just pretending it isn't there."

That was the only partly true thing I'd heard Kate say, but I wasn't about to agree with her.

"Whatever. I avoid conflict, then. Add it to my list of character flaws," Spinky said. "This is finished, though. Leave Moxie alone. The stuff she told me that wasn't true is between her and me, period. And whatever you thought she said to me about your family, you made a mistake."

Kate looked genuinely pained for a moment.

"You . . . but you . . . I asked if you wanted to go to Van Kempen and Crumble to check out their sale. And you said, 'I'm not like you—I can't shop there.' Then you gave me this look and said, 'And don't tell me you don't know what I mean.'"

Spinky gave Kate an astonished look, then let out a short, loud laugh.

"Kate, are you serious? Van Kempen and Crumble never stocks anything above a size four—it's like, their motto or something. I can't fit into their clothes. That's what I was talking about."

"You . . . but . . . you made that crack about *The National Enquirer*," Kate muttered.

"Yes, when I was explaining that I don't talk trash about people. Were we having the same conversation? I'm not going to tell you again—I don't do conflict. Take it somewhere else."

Kate looked like she was grasping for words. I stared at her. I was past the point where I thought I might cry. Now I just felt sick, and mad.

"Forget it," Kate said. "None of it matters anyway. I'm just going to end up at a new school again, as usual, so what's the point."

Then she stormed out through the open door like she was the one who'd just been publicly humiliated.

I felt the sudden need to sit, and since there was no furniture nearby, I sat on the floor.

"So," Spinky declared, plopping down next to me. "*That* happened."

I buried my face in my hands.

"Don't play into Kate's hostility," Haven said, sitting down on the other side of me. "This is her negative karma playing out, not yours."

"No," I said. "It's mine too. You guys, I am so sorry I lied to you. I brought this all on my own head because

I decided when I came to Eaton I wouldn't be my boring self anymore."

"The Buddhists believe that attachment to self is the root of all suffering," Haven said gently.

"Then I must either be a very good Buddhist, or the worst one ever," I told her.

"Well, you're a good *roommate*," Spinky said. "And it isn't like you set out to hurt anybody."

They were both being so nice. I didn't deserve it. I didn't want anyone to be nice to me at the moment—not until I could get the sick feeling out of my stomach, and the panic out of my heart.

"I have to go," I said.

And I was out of the room in a flash, running, getting away from my troubles as fast as I could.

Chapter Seventeen

My feet knew where I was going before my mind did. There are places everyone goes instinctively when they need to be completely safe. My father was at home alone once and got struck by lightning while he was walking out to our garage. He said he didn't remember anything that happened for the next ten minutes but he woke up in his own bed. His brain was temporarily scorched, but his feet automatically knew where he needed to go and got him there.

My feet took me, in record time, to the small piano in Sage Living Room. The practice rooms, the music wing itself, were too far away. I usually avoided the Sage piano so that people wouldn't wander by and hear me, but I needed to play now. I played Béla Bartók first, because his pieces—Miss Nimetz had forced me to memorize some of them to exercise my fingers—make me mad, and I was so furious at Kate Southington, I felt like the top of my head was going to blow off. My fury was only increased by the knowledge that I was not an innocent, wrongly blamed victim, and that Kate was right—I had been deceiving people, both people I didn't know well and those I now considered my friends.

I hadn't started out thinking what I was doing was lying, but not even the biggest blob of Mr. Tate's good mayonnaise could disguise this. I had lied. And though my intentions had not been bad, the results were. Especially where Reagan was concerned. All I wanted was to take advantage of the opportunity to reinvent myself. Now I had blown the chance, been publicly humiliated, and hurt one of the people that had become the most important to me at Eaton.

I abandoned the Bartók mid-measure and switched to Bach, because I needed to think logically. What did this all mean? What was my next move? My Eaton life was basically over. I felt like such an idiot. Why not just tell my parents the boarding school thing wasn't working out, and go home? That offer had been on the table from the beginning, after all. I could live at home forever, growing white-haired and teaching piano and taking in stray cats until the neighborhood children started weaving tales of my tragic past and my story was adapted for Lifetime Television.

I stopped just a few lines into the Well-Tempered Clavier and launched into Beethoven's Moonlight Sonata instead, because now I felt so highly emotional, I could hardly stand it. I didn't *want* to leave Eaton. I loved it here. I loved Spinky, and Haven, and Reagan, though they were so different from one another. I wanted to spend the next five years with them. And with Ms. Hay. And I could hardly imagine piano lessons without Mr. Tate. But how could I stay? Reagan might never talk to me again. Kate was probably already broadcasting what had just happened to the four corners of the earth. How could I hold my head up now? I was the Dope of the Decade.

My fingers moved almost by themselves while my ears and heart listened. The first movement of the Moonlight Sonata always made me cry. I played the two final, quiet chords, then just sat there looking at my hands until I heard someone breathe out very quietly, in a tiny muffled sigh.

Spinky was standing in the doorway of Sage Living Room, her mouth hanging open.

"How could I have not known about this?"

I ducked my head.

"The Personality Log?" I mumbled.

Spinky made an exasperated sound and rushed into the room.

"No, *this!*"

She grabbed my hand and plunked it onto the keys.

"What? I play the piano," I said as Spinky slid onto the piano bench beside me.

"You play the piano," Spinky repeated. "Yes. Johnny Depp acts. Donald Trump makes money. You play the piano. I knew you took lessons. But Moxie, you're amazing! How could I have not known you could play like this?"

I shrugged.

"How did you know I was here?" I asked.

"I followed you. I was worried when you rushed off like that. I had no idea where you were going. I came down the stairs after you, and you came in here. And then I hear this beautiful music—Moxie, you play like one of those concert player people!"

"No, I don't," I said. "Believe me, that wasn't as good as it sounded. Anybody could do that."

Spinky slapped one hand against her forehead, then nudged me with her shoulder.

"Mox, please. You're like one of those little music geniuses that goes on the Ellen talk show."

I shook my head.

"I'm really not a music genius, Spinky. Trust me—I've met a few. Yes I can play some things well, but so can thousands of other people. It's very ordinary."

Spinky laughed.

"That. Was not. Ordinary," she said. "What you just played . . . What was it, anyway?"

"Beethoven's Moonlight Sonata. But that was only the first movement. Someone super-good could play the third movement to tempo."

"Why? What's so special about it?"

I sighed.

"It's . . . you know. I'm sure you know it. It's famous for being hard. It starts like this . . ."

I played a few lines from it, wincing at every mistake. My rendition would certainly have made Beethoven relieved to be deaf. I stopped playing, and Spinky let out a soft whoop.

"Wow!" Spinky said, clapping her hands together. "That was incredible!"

I shook my head.

"No, Spinky, seriously. It's supposed to be played almost

twice that fast. And I make mistakes all through—you just don't know the notes well enough, so you don't notice. Maybe if I took six months and worked with Mr. Tate I could get it. Anybody could if they were willing to put in the zillion hours slogging it out. I'm enough of a doofus to spend that many hours in a practice room. Anybody could do it. You could."

Spinky stared at me with a wild grin on her face. Then she cracked up, still looking at me.

"Okay, Mox, let me get this straight. You only sound like a fantastic musician—but you aren't actually one—you're just a boring person who spends too much time in the practice room, which anyone could do."

"I'm just saying it's way more boring than you think— plenty of people can play better than I can, and I can play what I play because I'm a music nerd and I have nothing else to do with my free time but practice."

"Yeah? Does music nerd show up in your Personality Log anywhere?"

I groaned.

"Of course not. That's part of the personality I was trying to get away from."

"Why?"

I stared at her. She looked genuinely perplexed.

"Why?" Spinky repeated. "Why wouldn't Eccentric Gifted Music Genius make it onto your list? It sounds pretty cool."

"That doesn't really describe me. And it isn't especially cool either."

"You don't get to decide that," Spinky said. "I stood here and listened to you play Beethoven. I'm here to tell you, it was cool."

"I made mistakes. Even if you didn't hear them, the truth is I make mistakes even in the easy movement."

Spinky nudged my shoulder, still grinning.

"Moxie, you don't need Yoda to waddle through the door and extract the obvious wisdom here. Everybody makes mistakes. I make fantastic ones. Look at this."

She showed me a small tattoo on her arm, a word comprised of several Chinese characters.

"You think getting a tattoo was a mistake?" I said.

"Nope. I love my tattoos. But I wanted to save money, and I went to this totally cheap place to get this one. I wanted the word PEACE written out in Chinese. The guy had a book—he looked it up. But Helen Cho, this girl in my grade from back home, told me the guy got it wrong. Way wrong."

"It doesn't say peace?"

"Nope. It says DISCO."

I laughed.

"I know, right? Pretty big mistake. Not that anyone would know if I didn't tell them. But actually, I think it's hilarious. It's so me, you know? A total Spinkyism."

I laughed again, looking at that cryptic tattoo. Then my short-term memory came back, and I looked down.

"Do you think I should leave school?" I asked.

"Leave school as in run away?" Spinky asked, astonished. "What, did the circus make you a better offer?"

"I'm a laughingstock at Eaton now."

Spinky gave me a frank look.

"You're a funny girl, Moxie," she said. "I've never met anyone who cared so much about what people thought of her. And then you have this incredible talent, which you basically hide so people will think you're something else. You've got to give up trying to control that. You can't *tell* anyone 'This is who I am.' We'll all figure it out by ourselves. I have."

I peered at her, my hair hanging in my face.

"You have?"

"Of course. You're a creative person with a very kind heart, a great sense of humor, a flair for the dramatic, and a wide variety of interests. Not to mention being able to play amazing things on the piano. And apparently, you have this tiny obsession with being different people depending on who you're talking to . . . and there's only two ways out of that."

"What are they?"

Spinky stood up.

"Get over it, or check yourself into the nuthouse."

Option one, on the whole, looked like the better choice to me.

Chapter Eighteen

I'd like to be able to report that word did not spread about my Personality Logbook, so that I was left to absorb the lesson I had learned in my own good time.

I'd like to be able to tell you that. But I can't. Kate didn't have all that many friends. In fact, I don't know who she even liked other than Spinky. But the word had managed to spread itself to a few people, who spread the word to a few more, and you know how that goes.

I worked on Variation 28 constantly. I had a day and a half until the talent show, and now more than ever I was sure it was what Mr. Tate hoped and believed I would perform.

I'd also finally taken to heart Ms. Hay's advice that one

should never put off till tomorrow what one can do today. I outlined a supposedly comic presentation for the talent show. It was light, corny, glib, and could not be less representative of what I'd really learned in EE, and at Eaton. I hated it.

If I was really going to put the whole Personality Log behind me, if I was really going to just be Moxie Roosevelt Kipper, with all her wrinkles and karmic zits, I was going to have to abandon my talent show comedy outline. I knew that. But I had no idea what to put in its place. I was just going to have to rely on faith—or dumb luck—that something would come to me.

"There is nothing wrong, I promise," I said, shifting the phone to my other ear.

"I don't understand, then," my mother said. "Why in the world don't you want us to come?"

"I do want you to come," I insisted. "Just not for the Open Visit weekend. I have to get up in front of the entire school and perform."

"Exactly," my mother said. "We want to be there for you, Moxie. You know I've never missed one of your recitals."

I hadn't told her I was considering tackling 28. If I had a shot at convincing her not to come to the talent show, she'd have to think the piano part was totally unimportant.

"But this isn't some big recital, Mom," I said. "You've heard me play the Goldberg Variations a hundred times. That part's going to be fine. But like I told you, I have to get up there and supposedly be funny and talk about myself."

"Moxie, what exactly could you say about yourself in front of the entire student body that you don't want me to hear?"

I took a deep breath.

"It's not that I don't . . . I can't really— Mom, listen. It's not what I'm going to say, so much as how . . . I'll tell you all about it once it's over. It's not even finished yet—I don't even know what I'm going to say, exactly. I'm just stressed out, and I'll be more stressed if I know you're coming out to see it."

"Moxie, I don't see the problem. What would I see that would cause you stress? You haven't lost a limb or something, have you? Oh my gosh, I know what it is."

"Mom . . ."

"You've dyed your hair like that Sporky girl, haven't you? That's what this is all about. Moxie, I—"

"Mom! It's Spinky, first of all, not Sporky, and certainly

not 'that Sporky girl.' And no, I haven't done anything to my hair. Or lost a limb," I added.

"If you're under stress, I can help you, Moxie. I'll come and bring some—"

"Mom!" I said too loudly. Then I took a breath. "Mom," I said, in my best quiet and reasonable tone. "I am appealing to you as my mother. The thing is, I was kind of stupid my first month at Eaton. I did some things that weren't so great."

My mother took a deep breath—the kind she usually reserved for the editorial page of the *New York Times*.

"Moxie, are you in trouble? You haven't been . . . Did you—"

"I haven't broken any rules," I said quickly. "Or even laws, for that matter. I'm not in that kind of trouble. I just . . . I sort of made myself out to be somebody I'm not. And now I'm trying to find my way back."

"Sweetie, why would you make yourself out to be anything other than the extraordinary girl you are?"

I sighed.

"Conversation for another time, maybe. Like, when I've figured out the answer. But in the meantime, I have to do this stupid talent show thing and it's embarrassing, okay? And I just need some space for it. It's kind of like the changing room at Macy's. I can try the dress on, but I really need to get out of my old outfit without you watching me."

"I don't know," she said. "It sounds like the subtext is that you need me more than ever."

Ack. Would she ever relent?!

"No subtext, Mom," I said, trying not to sound exasperated. "I promise you I will give you an absolutely faithful blow by blow once it's all over. But please. Please please. Let me fly solo on this one."

There was a silence. I could practically hear my mother chewing on her lower lip—a classic sign of indecision.

"You know, Moxie, that you're a very special . . . That is, it isn't just because I'm your mother that I think . . . You are a person with many special gifts, and . . ."

"Mom."

"Moxie."

"Mooooommmmm. . . ."

She sighed.

"All right. On one condition."

"Name it," I said eagerly.

"Don't make up your mind today. Give it twenty-four hours. If you still feel the same way, your father and I will respect your wishes."

"Thank you, Mom," I said, biting back sudden tears. I

was relieved . . . and more terrified than ever. She could have her twenty-four hours. I wasn't going to change my mind. I was officially on my own.

"Twenty-four hours. I want your promise, Spanky Cheeks."

When in extremity, it is wise to permit parents to verbalize the most excruciating of nicknames without objection. I swallowed the rising lump in my throat.

"I promise, Mom."

"And I don't even want to think about how I'm going to explain this to your father."

"He's a guy, Mom," I said, finally pulling it together. "He's not detail-oriented. I bet he won't even ask. He'll probably think it's boy-related."

"There are no boys at Eaton."

Except for Luscious Luke.

"Okay, but still."

"Twenty-four hours, Mox," she said.

"You are an outstanding parental paradigm," I declared.

"Mmmm. So I'll hear from you tomorrow?"

"You'll hear from me tomorrow. Kipper to Kipper."

She sighed.

"Okay, sweetheart. Make sure I do."

"Love you, Mom."

"Love you too, Moxie Roosevelt. Good night."

I hung up, shaking but relieved. I had now removed one of two major obstacles to my Self-Confidence Through Comedy presentation.

The second being that I needed a plan B, and I didn't have one.

Chapter Nineteen

I kept carrying around my old outline—the one I'd written that I now couldn't bear the nightmarish thought of using. Even the night before the show I had it folded up in my pocket, making a little square dent in my jeans. For the last few days, every time I started thinking about standing up there with my awful bubble-gum-wrapper jokes, I'd freak out and run to the practice rooms to hide between the keys.

Tonight—my last night—was no different. I'd been lying low during dinner, trying to study for my algebra midterm, when my mind started picking over the same scab. When I got to my favorite practice room, I slid onto the bench and warmed up my fingers with some scales and chord progressions. The chatter in my mind fell away to the single focus of fingers on keyboard. It was the day before the talent show. If I was going to be able to play Variation 28 correctly to tempo, I had to be able to do it now.

I began to play.

I chased my thoughts away as Haven had taught me in meditation, and played without thinking. And it worked. It worked like a charm. Twenty, forty, eighty bars in and the music was flowing, my trills were fluid, my eighth notes to speed. I was playing it perfectly! I was doing it! At least, I was doing it until the thought that I was doing it appeared in my mind. Suddenly I became more focused on the thought than the music. *I'm halfway through Variation 28 with no mistakes* was flashing like a strobe in my mind. Please, no mistakes! What about that tricky hand crossover in the section where—

I hit a wrong note, then two more, and suddenly the flow I had found a minute before was gone.

I balled my hands into fists and struck the keys, taking pleasure in the sound of the musical bang.

It wasn't that I couldn't do it. There wasn't a section in the piece I now could not play through. I just had to stop my mind from jumping in and ruining it. Could I get up in front of the whole school and play Variation 28 the way I knew I could play it? Could I face Mr. Tate if I flaked out and played something easier—something safer? I could live with not knowing for sure what piece I was going to play . . . Music was music and some part of me believed it would all work out the way it was meant to, because it always did. I allowed myself that second of relief, only to be blindsided by the limp and stale noodle of my supposed comedy routine rearing its ugly head.

Would anyone, at this point, even care what I said?

But I had to try. And I was out of time.

For better or worse, in sickness or in health, till death do I fall apart, the reinvention of Moxie Roosevelt was about to reach its finale.

I had a piano lesson the morning of the talent show. Mr. Tate didn't mention my upcoming performance. Even more surprisingly, he didn't ask me to play the variation to start the lesson. He didn't ask me to play anything at all. Instead, he wanted to show me something.

"I'm an old-fashioned fella," Mr. Tate said, fiddling with a laptop computer, "and I can honestly say, Miss Kippah, I'd be happy enough if we were still using stone knives and bearskins to write things down. But every once in a while these computer machines get my attention. And an old student of mine sent something along that got my attention. Watch this."

Mr. Tate hit a button and everything disappeared from his computer screen except for a painting of the composer Franz Liszt, his face wild and glowering.

"Whoops," Mr. Tate said. He hit another button. Part of the score of Mahler's Resurrection Symphony appeared.

"I'm all turned around now," he muttered. "I know it's in here somewhere."

He peeked around behind the computer, like part of whatever he was looking for might be hanging out of the back of the screen. He shook his head, and tapped the keys again.

"Well now, that's better," he said. "It's our friend Mr. Kempff," he told me. "Did you know these machines could work just like a television? I just press this triangle, here, and it goes. I have seen many things, but I have never seen this footage. This may be one of the last times Mr. Kempff was ever recorded playing. He must be seventy-five or eighty years old here."

I scooched my chair closer to the computer and watched.

Kempff was beginning the slow, languid movement of

Beethoven's Moonlight Sonata. As he played, he lifted his head and gazed off into the distance. His pale blue eyes were so intelligent, so soulful. As the camera lingered on his face, it was as if his playing were as much a part of him as his breathing. He seemed to give it barely any thought, only occasionally casting a quick glimpse at the keys. Otherwise it was as if the music had sent him far away and followed him there. His hands looked old. His face was wrinkled and mottled, his hair wispy and gray. He was no picture-perfect display of good looks, and yet his face while he played was one of the most wonderful things I'd ever seen.

Neither of us spoke until the entire video had played, through the brief second movement and the frantic explosion of the third.

"What a privilege," Mr. Tate said, "to see an old master play Beethoven as if the music was the only thing keeping his world together. Not as fast as he played it in his prime, not as sharp. But I like this better. Everything he lived, all his experiences, is right there in the notes. Especially the ones he can't make his fingers play anymore."

We worked with my own Beethoven for the rest of the lesson, and I wondered how I would play the Moonlight Sonata in sixty or seventy years. I didn't voice the thought to Mr. Tate, nor did I express any of the anxiety I felt about the evening's performance.

And he, for whatever reason, didn't ask.

By the time my name was called at the New Student Talent Show that evening, I had a serious case of nerves. And that was putting it mildly.

Everyone I knew, and everyone I didn't, was in the audience. Spinky and Haven sat with me in the front row, quietly encouraging me, each in her own way. Reagan had not spoken to me in the days since my sea cow deception had come to light. Sage had given a few friendly waves across the dining hall, but she was clearly sticking with Reagan. I had seen absolutely nothing of Kate Southington. She could not have kept a lower profile had she been taken into the Witness Protection Program.

I couldn't do it.

I had to do it.

Couldn't.

Had to.

Spinky gently nudged me.

"They're calling your name, Moxie from Biloxi," she said, giving me a reassuring squeeze on the arm.

I had never felt this terrified before getting on a stage.

Then again, I had never faced a performance like this one.

I got up, took a moment to make sure I wasn't going to plummet to the floor in a dead faint, and made my way out of the row of seats and up the stairs to the stage.

"Hi. I'm Moxie Roosevelt Kipper."

A sea of faces stared at me, rows and rows of blurry ovals, one indistinguishable from the next. I felt an uncomfortable silence peppered with a few snickers. A smattering of clapping came from Haven and Spinky's direction, and from somewhere in the back. The auditorium was dim, and the lights onstage were bright. It took a moment for my eyes to focus. When they did, I thought I saw Luscious Luke in the third row. I shifted my gaze to the front row where I had been sitting, and spotted a familiar tuft of green hair. I focused on the green.

The microphone was set a little too high, and I had to readjust it to bring it closer to my mouth. This immediately made me think of Ms. Hay, which made me feel a tiny bit braver. I had to plunge in.

"I'm, um . . . Moxie Roosevelt," I said, remembering with a flash of heat that I'd already covered that. My voice sounded too loud and too high over the PA system. I took a step back from the mike. Maybe too far. I leaned in. "I'm here because of . . . for two things."

People started shouting that they couldn't hear. I took a half step closer to the mike.

"I'm here for two things. For Self-Comedy Through . . . Oh, sorry. For Self-Comedy . . .

Someone groaned and turned it into a laugh. The laughter grew. I was already tanking. I sought out the tuft of green hair again, and could see that Spinky was clapping

"For my EE, Self-Confidence. Through Comedy. And for the music compartment. I'm also here for the music compartment."

Silence.

"Department," I corrected.

"Go Moxie!" Spinky called.

It had been a boisterous evening so far, with students shouting out various things, mostly supportive or humorous, as their classmates performed. Now I feared they were ready to roast someone.

"Yeah, go Moxie," echoed someone else. "Away!"

My face burned. One day this whole experience will just be another wrinkle, I told myself, thinking of Wilhelm Kempff's ancient, lined face. Just another wrinkle.

The program said that I was supposed to do my comedy piece first, and an unspecified piece on the piano at the end. My comedy outline was still folded up in my jeans pocket. But my hands were shaking so badly I wasn't sure I could even hold on to it.

My eye went to the piano, sitting there like a lifeboat on the large stage. It was the only chance I had to sidestep this *Titanic* of a disaster.

A moment later I found myself dragging the mike stand with me toward the piano, creating a screeching feedback sound over the PA that made people groan again. I sat down at the piano and played a soft scale. My palms were sweaty, and I had to wipe them on my pants, which I'm sure everybody noticed. It was too late to care what people thought now. I began to play the piano for real. I started the Goldberg Variations at the very beginning.

The sound of the notes, and the familiar feeling of the keys beneath my fingertips, soothed me. My racing heart slowed just a little. I tried to block out every portion of my reality except for the music. Bach starts the whole series of pieces with just one melody, then he adds to it and changes it around and makes different things out of it. Each one is a different variation. And if a person didn't know, they might never realize all the variations came from the same original theme. But they did.

My hands froze mid-note.

Oh my god.

This was . . . This was just what I'd done.

This was just like me.

I knew most of the Goldberg Variations inside and out. I had lived with them almost every day for over a year. How could it never have dawned on me? All that flailing around, all that trying on new personalities, layering them on top of each other. Over each other. Over *me*. I was like Bach's variations. No—my *personalities* were like Bach's variations, and I . . . I was the theme. I was all of it.

My head felt suddenly light as air, like it might float up and up and up to the stage lights.

I had never really gotten away from the music at all. I just didn't realize it until I stopped playing the personality game. Until I stopped *playing*. My heart started rapidly thunk-thunking again, and I felt my face flush.

The key to plan B was right here, in Johann Sebastian Bach.

I was still sitting there with my hands frozen above the keyboard. The entire auditorium had fallen into utter silence, the kind that indicates mass realization that a 100 percent authentic disaster is about to unfold. But I hadn't made a mistake. I had finally gotten it *right*. Like a bolt of lightning from the sky, I suddenly understood.

I bent the mike stand down close to my mouth, then

picked up playing where I left off. When I was finished, I spoke.

"That's how Bach opens the Goldberg Variations. With the melody he uses to build everything else on. The aria."

"The disaster aria," a voice called, and there was a burst of laughter followed by some shushing from various teachers standing against the wall. My stomach squeezed in on itself in a sickening spasm.

Just another wrinkle.

"That aria is the foundation that the thirty variations are built on. In the variations, sometimes you can still hear the aria, and sometimes they sound like totally different pieces. But they're not. They're all modifications of an original. Which brings me to an important point."

Thankfully, no one could think of a wisecrack to shout here. I was immensely grateful for this small mercy. I pulled the mike a little closer.

"Some of you know, and hopefully some of you don't know, that when I got to Eaton I decided to reinvent myself. I wanted to go from being a regular individually wrapped slice of American cheese to something much fancier. Something worthy of my crazy name. Something imported, say, maybe in the Stilton family."

Now there was dead silence. I'm sure that no matter

what these people were expecting, they weren't expecting me to tackle my personality issue openly, or compare it to cheese. I plowed ahead.

"My first big mistake in a series of spectacular mistakes was thinking it was possible to change the way people see you. You can't. Kind of like Bach can't control whether you like his aria or not."

I played the tune of the aria again.

"So let's say this is the personality I arrived with at Eaton. We'll call it, as one of you so aptly pointed out, my disaster aria."

There were a few chuckles.

"And that's where the first variation of Moxie comes in. My roommate has green hair and an eyebrow ring, right? In reality she's a total sweetheart, but she looks really tough. And I wanted to be just like her. So I went for Detached, Unique, and Coolly Knowing Moxie. Code name: DUCKI. And let's say for the sake of argument, it sounded something like this."

I took a deep breath and flexed my fingers before beginning Variation 1. Unlike the aria, this piece was fast and tricky. The right hand is nonstop melody going all over the place, and the left hand is making these logical but potentially lethal jumps from key to key at different intervals. It's short, but it takes a lot out of me. I got through it with only a few fudges. I got more applause. People like the fast, technical stuff.

"Yeah. So that's totally different, right? It's flashy and unique, and it gets your attention. But it's still something created out of the core aria. When I play something this technical, it sounds much more complicated than it is. It's just the tempo that's jacked up, really. The rest is just hours in the practice room. I finally get most of them right. Everything is DUCKI."

There were a few more laughs at this. I might have won a small handful of them over, but it didn't even matter. Whether they were with me or against me, I was going to say what I had to say.

"Then I met this other girl. She's completely different from my roommate, but she's really cool. For starters, she's a Buddhist, and she knows a lot about meditation and calming the mind. She's an amazing person, and I wanted to be like her too. Before I knew it, I had become Mysterious Earth Goddess Moxie. Code name: MEG. And in the process of becoming a MEG, I started saying things about myself that weren't really accurate. I *wanted* them to be true. I wanted to chant, and be a vegetarian, and have a guru. But the fact is, they *weren't* true. I was making them up. I couldn't be farther from DUCKI at this point. I wanted to be full-on MEG. And let's say the musical version of that sounds something like this."

I begin to play Variation 15, which had become one of my favorites. It's quiet and emotional, and sometimes I feel like it comes off as more human than some of the other variations. I wait when I'm finished, because people seem determined to clap after each one.

"So it's beautiful, right? Really different from 1 though. This one seems to tell a story, and I find it really spiritual and dreamlike. Really contemplative and sweet. If the Goldberg Variations were religious, I'm sure that Variation 15 would be a Buddhist."

A little more laughter. They weren't rolling in the aisles, but they weren't throwing tomatoes either. And they were attentive when I was playing. You can always tell when an audience is listening. This one was.

"So you can probably see where I'm going with this. I met a third girl who I liked a whole lot. She's an activist, actually. Not the kind who makes a five-dollar donation and wears a Greenpeace button on her jacket for three years. This girl is the real thing. She's committed. She takes action. She's incredible. Now, when I talk to this girl, I'm blown away. She's got petitions and articles. She's got plans. She's going to save the animals, and I realize I've always wanted to save them too. New Variation. I'm Assertive Revolutionary Activist Moxie. Code name: ARA."

I placed my hands back on the keyboard. Then paused, taking another deep breath. Everything was coming together. Sitting at the keyboard while I talked to the entire school made me feel safe. A little happy. I was almost enjoying myself. Almost.

"This is a new side of me I'm discovering. There's little components of the DUCKI me, and MEG me, but they've become this new creature—this entirely new piece. Kind of like Bach's Variation 21."

I start right in, relishing the dramatic, slow opening. It's practically half the speed of some of the pieces, but there is so much to fit in between the notes.

"If you hear what I hear, then you picked up on the compassion in that variation," I said. "It's slower and not so showy, but there's so much power there—it's like, unrelenting. Impossible to ignore. And incredibly important—just like she is."

I didn't even know if Reagan was in the audience, but I needed to say these things.

"So all this time, while I'm trying to escape my disaster aria, I'm trying out these DUCKIs and MEGs and ARAs, and there were a few others too."

"YankEES!" I hear called from somewhere near the back.

"Thank you, Lupe," I said, laughing. "So I wish I could wrap this up as neatly and as brilliantly as Bach wraps up the Goldberg Variations. But I can't. Because the fact is, my disaster aria morphed into a full-blown disaster when someone found the notes I'd been keeping about my different personalities, keeping track of what I'd said to who. And some of the people in that book found out I hadn't been honest with them. Actually, let's just call it what it is. I lied."

The room fell mostly silent.

"It was not a great moment in my personal history. There were a couple of people who didn't seem to mind so much that I'd said things that weren't true. But there were others, one very important person in particular, who were really hurt by what I had done. And I found out there wasn't much I could do, at least at the time, to make it better. So, realizing I've strayed a bit from the music and humor portion of the evening—apologies to Mr. Tate and Ms. Hay—I want to take the opportunity right now to tell all of you that I did something stupid and unnecessary, and it was my fault and no one else's, and I'm sorry."

"Go Mox!" Spinky called. I smiled at her.

"For those of you I haven't yet personally spoken to,

I have some announcements. And for the record, I don't mind if you all laugh. Because some of them are kind of funny, I realize. Doreen Doggit—are you here?"

I saw a hand shoot up.

"I never attended the Olympic trial spelunking finals. Black-haired girl who eats lunch with Mavis every day? Yes, you. Hi. I have not in fact been pursued by a barracuda while snorkeling. Charnay from South Africa? Yup—I have never seen a poltergeist levitate furniture."

I sighed through some moderately loud laughter. I was almost done.

"Haven?"

Haven waved at me.

"I don't know what Wiccans do, I'm not sure what a guru is, and I've never chanted. But I'll be up at dawn to meditate with you if you'll have me."

"Right on," Haven called.

"Spinky," I said, and I couldn't help reflecting her grin. "As we have discussed, I do not have a parole officer. I have never broken the law. And I currently have no plans to tattoo a cockroach onto my forearm."

Spinky flashed me the peace sign and called, "Disco!" I grinned as the audience giggled. I was in the home stretch.

"And lastly, Reagan. I don't know if she's even here, and I know she already knows this. But I think all of you should know it. I was not the apprentice swabber on a sloop sailing to publicize the plight of the North Atlantic sea cow."

This got a loud laugh.

"No, but actually, listen. Reagan is starting a school club called Students for Animal Rights . . . It's a very important thing. She was going to call it Eaton for Animal Rights but she was afraid people would think they had to consume lots of calories to contribute."

More laughter.

"She is an outstanding person, and she's going to make a big difference in the world, and I hope you'll all give her your support. And I hope one day, she'll accept my apology and let me throw in my support too."

Everyone clapped. I scanned row after row for Reagan, but couldn't see her anywhere.

"So . . . I think—I hope actually—that I've covered all the bases, since Ms. Hay has already received my full confession regarding my not being Amish—"

I paused, as quite a few people seemed to find this hilarious. When I started talking again the words came faster and faster. I felt giddy—euphoric with the knowledge that I was almost done—that the hardest part was already behind me. And I was still here. And I was sort of—yes, I could hardly believe it—I was having a good time.

". . . and I know she'll want me to sum things up by stating what I've learned. So here's the thing I've realized—something uniquely, one hundred percent vintage Moxie Roosevelt Kipper. In Bach's work, the farther away he gets from the aria, the more obvious it is that the variations can't exist without that aria. In the end, everything goes back to the foundation Bach gives us in the beginning. The same applies to me. You can understand the piece best by listening to all thirty variations. But each one, even the few I've played tonight, give this great window to all the different places a genius like Bach can take one melody."

And all at once I knew I was going to do it. Without any introduction, or warnings about mistakes, or disclaimers of any kind, I launched into Johann Sebastian Bach's 28th Goldberg Variation. I didn't allow myself to think what I sounded like, or anticipate a particularly difficult section, or worry that I had played two, four, nine wrong notes. I simply plunged into the experience directly, my left hand dancing through the trills like a hummingbird hovering over bee balm. I thought of nothing while my right hand navigated the notes, bouncing over the left hand and back, over and back. There wasn't anything to it except everything. The minute I stopped resisting the hard parts so strongly, it all came together, imperfect and wonderful.

And when I had played the final notes, the entire piece taking only around two minutes, I put my hands in my lap. That was that. Nobody in the audience knew how long it had taken me to drum up the courage to even try to play this variation. How many hours of work I'd put in, how many mistakes were fudged into the lightning-fast trills. But it didn't matter. It was what it was. I was who I was.

I stood up and took the microphone in my hand.

"I'm Moxie Roosevelt Kipper, in I don't know how many crazy variations. One of the most important things I've learned from my music teacher here, Mr. Tate, is that I'll never be done as a pianist—I'll always have work to do. Now I realize that applies to all of me. And if Ms. Hay has taught me one thing, it's how to laugh at myself. Oh, and to always check your seams before doing Downward Facing Dog. Words to live by. Thanks."

I put the mike back on the stand and walked off the stage into the wings. People clapped, and I heard Spinky and Haven calling my name. Don't get me wrong—it wasn't thunderous applause. There was no standing ovation.

No one begged me to come out and entertain them some more. But they'd listened, and some of them had laughed. And they had seen me, just as I was.

The Reinvention of Moxie Roosevelt was over. And the real Moxie Roosevelt had finally stood up.

Chapter Twenty

Spinky found me backstage after the final act, where I had remained standing in a state of controlled post-talent-show paralysis. Spinky escorted me out the fire exit into the crisp night air by the auditorium parking lot, her arm linked through mine.

"You're quite a composer," she said, pulling her scarf around her neck and zipping her leather jacket up to her dimpled chin.

"That was a performance, not a composition," I corrected. My voice sounded weird all by itself, no longer channeled and amplified through the loudspeakers.

Spinky grinned.

"I think it could be argued either way," she said.

"Well, Moxie Roosevelt, as I live and breathe," I heard.

Ms. Hay was standing in the fire exit, illuminated from behind. She looked like an ethereal doorstop.

"Pass or fail?" I asked, my words fogging the night air.

She came outside laughing, and gave me a hug, the bobble on her hat coming just to the bottom of my chin. Someone else came into the doorway behind her.

"I had a feeling about tonight," she said.

"That sounds ominous," I said ruefully.

"No, I did," Ms. Hay insisted. "You're living proof that Self-Confidence Through Comedy is a valuable offering for students."

"You make it sound like I'm the first to pass," I said.

"You are the first at all," Ms. Hay said. "I had to face down the administration to get this EE approved. If you hadn't signed up, they would have canned it."

Wow. My clipboard malfunction had been responsible for more than I knew.

"Moxie—you're getting more auspicious by the minute," Spinky declared.

"Um, this is my roommate, Spinky Spanger."

Ms. Hay waved at Spinky.

"Your reputation precedes you, Spinky," Ms. Hay said.

Spinky bowed.

"So does yours. And not to rain on your EE parade, but Haven was supposed to meet us around front, on the quad," Spinky told me. "She's going to wonder what happened to us."

"Yeah come on, Hobbit," came a male voice from the doorway. My mouth almost dropped open. Was I dreaming, or had some random guy actually called Ms. Hay *Hobbit* out loud?

"Keep your hair on," Ms. Hay said, still grinning. "Moxie, this is my husband, Jim."

Husband? Ms. Hay had a husband? Why yes, there was a little ring on that tiny finger.

"Ah yes, the famous Moxie," said Mr. Hobbit, stepping out of the doorway and onto the grass. He was, if not tall, of perfectly normal height and exceeded average cuteness by a long shot. "Nice to meet you. Now if you'll excuse us, I'm going to remove Hobbit from the premises. There's a Bears game on TV tonight."

Ms. Hay rolled her eyes.

"He calls me Hobbit," she said. "I really have no idea why."

Then she flashed me the Vulcan finger sign, and followed her husband into the parking lot.

I stared after her for a moment. Ms. Hay was full of surprises.

Spinky pulled my arm.

"Ready?"

I nodded, and Spinky linked her arm in mine, walking me onto the path that led around the auditorium and toward the inner quad. I was in a daze, and let Spinky do the driving for both of us. I noticed someone walking toward us, but didn't register who it was until I heard a voice say my name. A male voice. Which is a sound that really gets one's attention at an all girls' school.

Spinky and I stopped, and I squinted into the distance. I had to be hallucinating.

"Hey Moxie," he said again as he pulled even with us.

It was Luscious Luke. And he was Luscious Luking right at me.

"Moxie Roosevelt, right?" he repeated.

"That's me," I squeaked.

"You're good on the piano," he said.

And then his legs transported the rest of his awesomeness down the path.

He knew my name. Luscious Luke *knew my name*. And I wasn't even wearing high bouncy pigtails. I would never think of Carson McGillion again.

Perhaps not entirely true.

"Come on, celebrity," said Spinky, pulling gently on my arm.

"Wait," I said. "I have to see if Mr. Tate has come out yet."

A few people were still exiting the auditorium. Mr. Tate was always easy to pick out, even in a crowd, and tonight was no exception. He was standing to the side of the door, his hair even wilder than usual. He looked like he'd been strolling casually through a wind tunnel. As I walked toward him, he checked his watch, looked surprised, and checked it again.

"Mr. Tate," I called, and he looked up. He was wearing the same green sweater he had on the day we had our first meeting, and khaki pants, and his spotless white Converse high-tops. His only concession to the cold October air was a maroon muffler wrapped several times around his neck.

"Ah, Miss Kippah. I thought perhaps you had been detained by your legion of fans at the stage door."

Stage doe-ah.

"I'm afraid not, Mr. Tate," I said. "Just my roommate."

He examined me silently for a moment. All the nervous talkie-fillers I might produce for someone else—"I'm sorry it wasn't . . . I hope you thought it was okay even though . . . I realize I should have . . ."—weren't necessary for Mr. Tate. There was nothing I could say to him that he didn't already understand about my music. Whatever embarrassing tidbits about the rest of my life that I'd just aired in the auditorium would not matter to him one bit.

"Well now," he said finally. "You hit one out of the park this evening, Miss Kippah."

I broke into a huge smile

"Thank you," I told him.

"Oh, it's my pleasure."

Mah pleh-zhuh.

"Go on now, and see your friends. You and I will get back to work on Monday morning," he said, adjusting his muffler and gazing off toward the dining hall, where he probably expected breakfast was now being prepared.

"I'll be ready," I said.

Mr. Tate laughed.

"Oh, I have no doubt you will. Good night, Miss Moxie Roosevelt Kippah."

Ki-puh. It actually sounded quite elegant when he said it.

"Good night," I said.

Spinky was waiting for me on the quad, which was filled with a large number of students, and a smaller number of parents. Conversation, hugs, and the occasional flash of cash were being exchanged.

"Are you wishing you parents had come after all?" Spinky asked, as if reading my thoughts.

I shook my head.

"No. I'm glad I asked them to sit this one out. I kind

of had to bare my soul a little in there, and I just couldn't have done it with my mom and dad watching," I said.

"I hear that," Spinky said. "Like when I had my eyebrow pierced."

I hugged her.

"Exactly like that, Spinky," I said.

"There's Haven."

Haven was sitting under a tree by the side of the auditorium, her long brown hair spilling out of a wool hat, looking peaceful and expectant, as if Buddha himself might descend on a moonbeam and scoop her up into the twilight at any moment. But instead of disappearing into nirvana, Haven caught sight of me and waved. And I noticed she wasn't alone.

I gave Spinky's arm one last squeeze, took a breath, and walked over to them.

"Reagan. Hi. I don't know if you were at the thing just now, but—"

"Technically, attendance was required for new students," Reagan said. She was looking at her hands. I glanced over at Haven, who smiled and mouthed, "Hi."

"Oh, right, okay. I won't keep you, I just . . . what I said, about being sorry. I really meant it."

Reagan remained fascinated with her hands, and I

turned to go. If I'd learned anything, it was that there was nothing I could say that could make Reagan change her opinion of me.

"Wait," Reagan said. I saw now that she was holding something in her hands, which she carefully handed to Haven. Then she pulled a folded-up piece of paper out of her pocket and held it up in her mittened hand for me to see.

"What is it?" I asked.

"An e-mail from Julius Severay, saying he'll be an honorary advisor of my animal rights club and he'll put a link to it on the Global Wildlife Coalition."

"Reagan, that's amazing!"

"Your mom really does know him. You really did ask her."

"Yeah," I said. "That part was true. Listen, I am SO sorry about the sea cows . . . about everything . . ."

"Julius Severay is a legend," Reagan said, staring at the paper. "This is huge. This is going to make a difference."

"I'm glad," I said. "I'm really glad."

"Outstanding," said Spinky. She was beaming, now that peace had returned to our little group.

"Now we need a terrarium," Reagan said.

"For . . . for the e-mail?" I asked.

Reagan pointed at Haven, who was holding both hands out in front of her like she was begging for a bit of bread.

"Meet Siddhartha," Haven said. "Reagan let me name him."

Spinky and I peered into Haven's hands. A tiny turtle sat motionless in her palms.

"I was walking Sage's parents to their car with her, because they wanted to take her to Pizza World," Reagan said, "and I found him halfway across the blacktop. Do you know how many cars are pulling out of that lot right now? He never would have made it."

"Wow, he's gorgeous," Spinky said. "Are we going to keep him?"

"We can't keep him," Reagan admonished. "He belongs in the wild. But I was thinking maybe he could hang with you and Moxie until we sort out a good place to release him."

"We'd love that," I said quickly. "I have a shoebox that would work until we can get something better. Siddhartha will be safe with us."

"I know that," Reagan said. She glanced at me, then returned her attention to the little turtle. I was learning enough about Reagan to guess that there was going to be no tearful hugging session right now—we would not be sitting up all night braiding each other's hair and giggling. But we were okay.

"Let's go then," I said. "Let's get Siddhartha into his bunk—he's probably stressed out."

"Let's just pick some grass for him, so he has some familiar smells around," Reagan said.

We were all three bending down to pull handfuls of grass when someone called out.

"There they are now—hey Spinky, Moxie!"

Our proctor, Kristen, was walking down the path, her hand on the shoulder of a girl I didn't recognize.

"Your Worthiness," Spinky called. "How might we assist you?"

"Very funny. This is Danni, your new roommate. She just got in before dinner—I left you guys a note."

Apparently Spinky had gotten her information wrong. This girl was about as goth as a Powerpuff Girl.

"We were getting ready for the show," I said. "Nice to meet you, Danni."

"Hi," said the girl. "Hey, I just saw you onstage. You're the Moxie."

"I am," I confirmed. "I am the Moxie."

She was a vision of sorts, in perfectly pressed jeans and a pink Lacoste shirt, collar flipped up, under a green down vest. She had large brown eyes and golden brown hair pulled back by a velvet headband. She looked like she'd just come from lunch at the yacht club. "And I am the Spinky," Spinky said.

"Spinky? Is that your real name?"

"As real as it gets," Spinky replied. "I heard you were totally goth. And that you made quite an exit."

Danni laughed. "Oh god, goth was *so* last year," she said. "And yes, I went to the science lab with a fever and ended up passing out on the floor. Mono is so contagious, they ended up sending me home."

That's what had caused the mysterious departure of Dannika Sorenson? Everyone will be so disappointed, I thought. People prefer window-shattering explosions and escaped killer viruses to simple truths.

"Danni, your parents are waiting in the administration office," Kristen reminded her. "I just thought I'd introduce you, since we were walking by. I'll bring Danni back up to the room before check-in."

Danni gave us a little wave, and I watched her walk off, her brown ponytail bouncing in tandem with Kristen's blond one.

"I guess we don't have to worry about Marilyn Manson posters," I said cheerfully as the four of us walked toward Sage.

"Hey, hang on, people," Spinky said. She pointed up to third-floor Sage at Haven's window. "Behold."

Two strings of silver wire had been slung through the little hooks that kept the windows from pitching out all the way when they were cleaned. The wires met halfway down the window and were wrapped around a bronze object that gleamed in the moonlight like the Holy Grail.

"You did it!" Haven exclaimed. "My incense burner!"

"It's a triumph of physics," Spinky said. "I even tried it out. You can drop the incense in, and the updraft brings the scent right back into the room. Plus, I had Kristen take a look. Miraculously, it doesn't violate the fire code."

"Thanks, friend," Haven said. "You rock."

"I do what I can," Spinky said modestly. "Let's go up, and I'll show you how to reel it in if you want to clean it."

"Guys, what's going on in the archway?" Reagan asked.

She pointed toward the stone passageway that separated the quad in front of Sage from the faculty parking area on the other side. A group of girls had gathered there, and a few of them were taking pictures.

"I hope nothing's wrong," Haven said.

"I hear laughing," I said. "Should we go look?"

"I'm taking Siddhartha upstairs," Reagan said. "Turtles don't like cold. Or crowds."

"I'm going inside too," Haven said. "There's a *Poltergeist* marathon on the Haunting Channel and I want to catch some of it."

I smiled at Haven. When it comes to personalities, one size definitely does NOT fit all.

"We'll be up in a minute," Spinky said. Haven pulled the heavy door open and held it for Reagan, who was holding her hands in front of her like she was carrying one of the crown jewels.

"Let's go see what all the fuss is about," Spinky said.

We made our way into the archway, where about fifteen girls were standing around staring at the parking lot. I instantly saw what had captured their attention—a white stretch Hummer limousine of revolting and improbable proportions occupying three faculty spots.

"Ew," I said. "Thank goodness my mother isn't here— she'd freak out if she saw that thing. She'd be homeschooling me by now."

"How do you park something like that?" Spinky wondered. "It must be like trying to dock an ocean liner."

I though I'd seen enough when three people pushed past me, enveloped in a cloud of expensive-smelling perfume. I caught sight of an unmistakable profile as they passed. Lockwood Southington, with a tall, nervously thin blond woman in a turquoise tweed pantsuit and white pashmina wrap, and a girl, hanging her head down so low her features were mostly invisible. But not to me.

"Oh no," I said.

"What?" Spinky asked. "Are you allergic?"

I guess she meant the perfume. I shook my head. There was no point in keeping the secret now.

"I think those are Kate's parents," I said.

Spinky squinted at the Hummer.

"What? Where? Do you see a police car?"

I shook my head.

"Her dad isn't a cop, Spinky. He's a hotel magnate—a billionaire. The Lockwood Southingtons. They're famous for being rich. Kate is one of *those* Southingtons."

"Uh-oh," Spinky said. "Not the background in law enforcement we were expecting."

"I have a feeling *she* wasn't expecting them at all," I said.

The inevitable moment arrived. Everyone was stopping to look at the Southingtons. Half the school had probably already seen Kate's parents. What was going through her mind?

I thought about it for a second. A person can go two ways after being publicly humiliated. You can be psyched that it's someone else's turn to be in the spotlight, or you can feel much worse for them than you might have thought possible. I was feeling truly dreadful for Kate Southington.

I realized Spinky was staring at me.

"Did you know?" she asked. Then she whistled under her breath. "That's what she thought you told me. You knew, didn't you?"

I shrugged.

"And you didn't tell—even when she came at you like that."

I shook my head.

"It just would have looked like I was trying to get back at her. And if you think about it, Spinky, insane as it seems now, I can understand how she wanted to pretend to be somebody else."

"Yeah, you said a mouthful," Spinky replied, casting a discreet look toward the flashy couple. "Listen, let's wait for her while she packs those people into their limo. She's going to need some friendly faces after her family takes off."

"You wait," I said. "I'm probably the last person in the world she wants to see."

Spinky laughed. "I think her parents are ahead of you on that list, Mox. Wait with me. If she tells you to buzz off, then you can. But the girl could probably use some friends around now. I think you might be a much more welcome sight than you think."

We stood off to one side of the archway on the parking lot side, stamping our feet to keep warm. Kate had pulled open one of the Hummer doors, and was looking at her feet as her parents continued to stand there. A uniformed driver appeared, looking flustered that one of his famous charges had performed his door-opening labor. Kate's father was talking, and her mother was smiling at the students who were still standing around, like she was having her picture taken for *People* magazine.

"I just wish I could understand why she started hating me so much in the first place," I said. "But she hated me on sight, before she thought I was going to tell her secret. She went through the stuff in my room—that's how she found my Personality Log. I guess she always planned on using it against me eventually. I still don't get it. I didn't even put her in the book."

Kate's mother now climbed daintily into the limousine, which I thought something of an accomplishment given her precarious, dangerously high heels.

"Maybe," Spinky said thoughtfully, "that was part of the problem. With her regular-person identity, she didn't even rate a mention in the Personality Log. Or maybe she just saw something in you she didn't like."

"What?" I asked.

"A person trying to reinvent herself. My granny says

sometimes the people that bug us the most are the ones who have faults we're secretly afraid we have too."

I considered what Spinky had just said as Lockwood Southington got into the limousine. As soon as the driver closed the door after him, Kate ducked her head and walked briskly toward the archway. She probably felt like half of Eaton had just seen the contents of her underwear drawer. I kind of knew how she felt.

Spinky was right. Kate and I, in our own bizarre way, were variations on a similar theme.

Kate almost walked right past us, head down, moving fast, but then she caught sight of Spinky.

"Hey," Spinky said. "Moxie and I are going to go raid the vending machines for some Twinkie therapy in our room. Want to come?" She said it casually, with no acknowledgment of what we'd all just seen, or the enormous SUV that was now navigating through the stone gates at the parking lot exit.

Kate hesitated, and took in my presence with a quick glance.

"Maybe some other time," she said to Spinky.

We made eye contact for the briefest of moments before she started moving away. There was nothing friendly in the look, but the raging hostility was gone. It was as if Kate had recognized the thing we had in common, and it had taken the venom out of her sting. We weren't going to be friends, but we didn't necessarily need to be enemies either.

"See you later," Kate said to Spinky, and she hurried off toward the Sage entrance.

"We tried," Spinky said. "I think she'll be okay. I'll check on her later. So how many quarters do you have?"

"How many quarters do I need?"

Spinky gave me her best leprechaun grin.

"How many Twinkies can you eat? Remember, it's Twinkie *therapy*. The more you eat, the more therapy you get."

And suddenly I realized I was starving. I could think of nothing better at this moment than retreating to the third floor of Sage to eat Twinkies with my strange and wonderful roommate. We probably made an odd-looking pair—me my usual unremarkable self, and Spinky with her dog collar and combat boots and the rest of the armor she wore every day.

"Do you think I should wear a dog collar?" I asked, only half seriously, as we headed back through the archway and into the school's side entrance where the vending machines were.

"It does have its advantages," Spinky said. "Nobody

knows what to make of you, which gives you just enough time to figure out what to make of *them*. Watch it work on our new roomie."

"I will," I said, laughing, though the thought of having a brand-new person living with me and Spinky was a little vexing.

Spinky Spanger and I went off to collect Twinkies and present ourselves to Dannika Sorenson, whose classroom fainting and infectious mono had mutated into a circus sideshow of rumors and theories.

Dannika would either like me or she wouldn't. All I had to offer her was myself—one fairly ordinary girl with a few special talents, and an already famous gift for variations, one who had been an actress, and the butt of a joke, and even kind of a criminal. Call it what you will, it was anything but boring.

Turns out I had some moxie after all.